Before *Stonewall!*
Before *"Woodstock!"*
Before "Hair" and *"Oh, Calcutta!"*
…there was "*ArtemisSmith's* **FOR IMMEDIATE DEMOLITION**"
Mass-Market Titled: "This Bed We Made"
JACK KALLISH

Get Ready for a REALLY WILD ROMP
In the pre-War 1960's!
MICHAEL MATTHIAS

"This is the book where it all began –
Where both 'Straights' and 'Gays' joined 'The Rainbow'
And worked together for World Peace and Gender Freedom!"
The Rev. MIKHAIL ITKIN

"When they make the film – I want the part!"

KAREN BLACK

For *Free Stuff* and a Continuing Web Experience
GoTo: http://ArtemisSmithMorpurgo.tripod.com/index.html

1965 AVANT GARDE MARATHON PHOTO BY JOHN GRAHAM

ArtemisSmith is a prominent strategist of the 1950-60's 'Unisex and Unirace' Rainbow civil rights coalition movements, activist co-author of *The Third Sex* and author of the pulp fiction best sellers *Odd Girl,* and *This Bed We Made.*

A contemporary of Andy Warhol and a still-living Poet, Philosopher, Playwright, Futurist and Digital Artist, in addition to operating her own successful off-Broadway workshop that gave rise to many of today's vintage Film and Television stars, she was the first Invited Speaker to tell the Gay Community at pre-Stonewall ECHO Conferences to look toward the Advertising Industry to change the Gay Image, and to hurry up and 'Come out of the Closet' or get left out of the civil rights *putsch.*

ArtemisSmith's

THIS BED WE MADE

(FOR IMMEDIATE DEMOLITION)

By Artemis Smith
(Annselm LNV Morpurgo a/k/a ArtemisSmith)

The Author's 2014 Re-Issue
Plus an Afterword and an Appendix containing
ArtemisSmith's "Hark the Pterodactyl"

Sag Harbor . New York . U.S.A.   ™

This Author's Re-Issue also contains a 2014 *Afterword* and a *copy* of ArtemisSmith's rare edition of "Hark the Pterodactyl" in the Appendix.

a Monograph of

THE SAVANT GARDE INSTITUTE

Academic Library Edition: ISBN 978-1-878998-31-6
LIBRARY OF CONGRESS CONTROL NO:2013958212

'the savant garde workshop' publishers
P.O.B. 1650 . SAG HARBOR . NEW YORK . 11963 . USA
Tel: 1.631.725.1414

1.

Except for the snoring bums who slept in doorways and behind empty trash cans, his street was deserted now on this dark fall morning, dank with the smell of garbage, soaked with fog. He stood for a moment taking it all in—the slum, the ruins of modern Pompeii, leaning out to him, welcoming him back, back to his home town, his Third Avenue just off the Bowery, New York, the greatest, stinkiest goddamn paradise in the world. It was good to be back.

He was a handsome man, not as tall as most but delicate-boned, porcelained, radiating wholesomeness in the meticulous neatness of his clothes. He carried a canvas suitcase—the kind bought at Walgreen's for airplane traveling.

"Beautiful goddamn heaven," he muttered involuntarily. He took it all in, stood there feeling loved by the smog as it caressed him damply through his light suit. Then a greater love drove him down a perilous set of steps to a dirty basement door. He unlocked it, then kicked it open, not bothering about the noise.

A multitude of paint cans barred his way to the middle of the long room where the living space had been kept clear. He knocked them aside and stood, watching, admiring with the eyes of an artist Elaine's trim ass. Or was it arse? It was beautiful, even without a name—white and firm, like the rest of her back, moled but not freckled and with the soft pencil lines of Michelangelo's men—not his burly women.

She was out. The kind of out that typified Elaine—unconscious, half dead, starved into a coma. He knew it wouldn't wake her for long but still he spoke her name. "Elaine."

He repeated it more emphatically: "Elaine!"

The sleeping nude stirred, slowly unwound herself out of the tangle of pillows and sheets she had embraced like a lover, slowly turned herself to unveil her soft white bosom with the wide, round, red nipples that seemed filled with wine.

"Elaine, it's Peter," he said.

"Peter?" She did not believe him. "Go away."

"Wake up," he insisted, taking a step nearer and daring to sit on the edge of her bed and to put his hand on her bare shoulder. He wanted to press his mouth to her breast but her own opened mouth confused him, made him unable to decide with which to begin. "I love you," he said instead.

"Screw you," she mumbled and turned face down again. He lingered for a moment, undecided, then proceeded to look after her. "A supreme self-sacrifice," he muttered to himself.

He went to the chair and took off his jacket, then rolled up his sleeves and found the kitchen.

It needed to be found like Heinrich Schliemann had found Troy—layer by layer. The stove was under a pile of dried paint palettes and the sink was loaded with cans of dirty turpentine. He wondered how she could have survived the whole year without him. She was at it again, slowly dying under the effort of giving birth. The brain child stood in the middle of the floor, waiting to be finished, waiting to finish Elaine. It was more than a painting this time—it was a monument to fear. Peter turned away and made coffee, dumping the accumulated debris from the stove onto the floor. Then, with domestic efficiency, he found a bowl of stale pancakes in the refrigerator, stuck behind a burlap-covered hunk of clay with a face like the painting—like Nicole. Peter wondered why Elaine was painting Nicole again, then shrugged and brought the pancakes and two cups over to the table and cleared a space. He wished he wouldn't have to feed her old pancakes but he was down to a dime.

He didn't hate her today. A year in San Francisco had cured him. All of a sudden the feeling had come over him that he should go back, that he had a wife and he wanted her. What a silly impulse. It had carried him three thousand miles. But it had been more than that. It had also been the nagging realization that he was getting to be thirty and still no clear sky above him; she was nearing thirty-two; they needed each other. He wished he could be tender about having come back, but she would think that "way out"—what, after a year of not hearing from him?—and so he tried to be cool speaking to her.

"Elaine," he said again, louder and with less respect. "Wake up. Coffee's on." He flicked on the ceiling light and also pulled the shades, opening the small cellar windows wide to let in the cold, damp air and smoke. "Come on, wake up," he snapped his fingers at her commandingly.

Still asleep, she sat up straight like a zombie, let him put the hot mug in her hand and gulped the coffee, punishing her throat with the scalding liquid.

He sat with his own cup and watched her, subtly devouring her with his eyes. She was lovely even now, with her hands stained and her arms splotched with the red pimples of turpentine allergy. She was discretely blond and her breasts had a classic droop, so did her stomach—starvation having made her flabby—was plump enough around the belly to give it the look of containing a womb. Her white legs were twisted in the sheets and her narrow feet folded in front of her with the innocent carelessness of a baby.

"Good morning, dear," Peter said in a tone that was almost mocking.

She shook the sleep out of her brain and looked at him. "What the hell do you want?"

"I thought I could borrow breakfast and a five." He said this innocently, with the supreme arrogance that he always used to his embarrassment. He hated asking her for money.

"I spent your last check," she grunted. "There's no breakfast."

"Wrong." He snapped his fingers playfully, then reached into the bowl for a pancake, a floppy one. He folded it and put it in her hand. She took it and bit into it hungrily, watching him help himself to a couple.

"Be my guest," she said. "It's the last of the box, I think."

"I see you're still starving," he said.

"By choice," she retorted.

"That's your hard luck, dear," he shrugged.

They were scratching at each other's being again, like a year ago, in a love-hate sort of way that had made them decide each morning that their marriage had to end. Peter stopped himself, stopped chewing the rubber pancake and paused to really look at Elaine's blue eyes. She was still an angel and her blond hair, a little darker than last year, glinted like fall grass in the light—slick and full of dance, full of the whisper of breezes.

After a while he spoke again. "Are John and Mirium still upstairs?"

She shrugged, "I guess."

"When did you last see them?"

"A month or two ago. I don't know." She yawned extravagantly and fell back on her pillow, her cup on her stomach. Her delicious breasts rose with her arms and she didn't care if he watched her. That was Elaine—not a whore at all, just unaware, her attention taken up by more important things than modesty.

"I'm staying for a while," he announced.

"Just don't mess up my work or I'll kick your teeth in," she mumbled, then rolled over into the same position in which he had first found her.

He stretched, breathed the smog and felt glad to be home, glad to be back in cruddy, corrupt New York. All the way on the plane he had asked himself, "*Quo vadis,* Peter?" And his answer had been, "To New York, to be crucified again."

But it didn't seem quite time for that now. He stood over nude Elaine and longed to take off his clothes and lie with her awhile, longed to feel the coldness of her white skin and to get inside her comfortably, not for much, for just a short caress, a sort of kiss, that's all. But it would cause her pain, would wake the awful gnawing ulcer in her belly and make it cry, "There's no room for you here. Wait till I eat more of her insides up—but she'll be too much in pain for you then."

He would have to feed her sour cream first, and her pills, then wait until she wanted him, until she would say, "Love me, even if it hurts—I don't care." He wondered if she would ever say that to him again. He tore away from the delicious agony of watching her and his eyes met the painting, the monstrosity that sat on the easel, blocking up the entire room. He stepped over to look at it—looking naked-eyed into the screaming sun of it, the awful burning clash of shape and color that somehow fit into a portrait pattern, a portrait of that woman Nicole.

Her coarse, peasant cheekbones were starkly real even through the cubic lines of Elaine's bold palette strokes. One thing was wrong with it, was new in Elaine's style—a million little details, pictures within the picture, busy patterns that had no place on the canvas, merely serving to confuse rather than add to the picture. That betrayed a lack of concentration on her part, an inability to organize and clarify. But it still had power. The background and Nicole's clothing were splashed with blood, red in the violent passion that throbbed through all of Elaine's work. The painting screamed at him and made him feel insanely jealous of its model and what she had meant to Elaine.

It was too late to go to sleep. Peter stretched again and finished his coffee, now cold like the morning, then retrieved his jacket and opened the warped door that led outside. He had a burning desire to see John and Mirium. He skipped up the steps of the building, kicked open the front door, then sprang up two more flights to the top where he heard peaceful snoring.

There was no door to John's apartment and Peter walked directly into the bedroom where he saw John's large bare stomach, hard like a pregnant giant's, protruding over the bed post. Mirium lay dwarfed in his arms, clothed in a sweat-filled slip, her long raven hair over her face. She was a light sleeper and she heard him.

"Pete, you old—" she sat right up and whirled her hair behind her, glad to see him.

He put his finger to his lips, shushing her, and tiptoed into the kitchen to repeat the coffee-making routine.

Mirium got up and slipped on a pair of John's old loafers and followed him, her hands folded around her shoulders for warmth. She was girlish, flat-chested, like a twelve-year-old and with a face unwrinkled by time, having a strange sort of ugliness that made her very beautiful. Her large black eyes betrayed a drop of Chinese blood from way back in her Irish-bohemian ancestry. She looked innocently at Peter now, in the first rays of sunlight coming through the windows. "Did you just get back?"

He nodded, puttering about. "I stopped at Elaine's." He felt at home here. John and Miriam were family to him, more than anyone else, more than Elaine even, because they liked him—really liked him without hate.

"Where have you been?" Miriam yawned, shaking off the hair which persistently got in front of her face.

"San Francisco, mostly," he said, spooning instant coffee into three cups, efficiently, like a waiter. "Has anything changed since last year?"

"Some, not much. I have a baby." She shrugged, routinely.

"Not really!" He whirled. "You weren't showing it when I left."

"Oh, it just dropped one day," she laughed. "She's still sleeping now."

He poured boiling water into the cups and the coffee was made. Mirium took John's cup and went in to wake him. He had rolled over on his side, causing Mirium's side of the bed to rise, seesawed way up in the air by his weight.

"John," Mirium spoke gently and placed the hot cup on the table, near his hand. "John." She bent over him tenderly and nibbled his ear, like a small fairy waking a giant.

"Huh?" John grunted and turned quickly on his back. She scrambled to get out of the way. "What's up?"

"Pete's here."

"Yes, Pete's here," Peter repeated, coming in and standing against the door, holding his and Mirium's cup. "Wake up, you old cyclotron."

"Pete!" John opened his eyes wide and sat up. "Man, welcome home!" With one motion he slid into his shoes and got up, pulling up his sloppy pajamas to warm his bellybutton.

"Sit down and drink your coffee," Peter said, walking to him. His manner was smiling but cold. He had never been able to show too much emotion, even in the throes of ecstasy. Here with John and

Mirium, things were close to ecstasy. "Are you eating these days?"

"Oh, sure," John hit his own stomach. "I got another grant."

Now Mirium came in with some stale coffee cake and they each took a slice. When John was awake Mirium said little, hovering about like a chambermaid, making herself useful.

"What can we do for you? Do you need a loan? You look thin, boy." John always spoke fast except when he was thinking.

"I could use five," Peter shrugged. "I need it for carfare and the want ads."

"Sure," John grunted, then turned to Mirium. "Hey, hon, raid the cookie jar for Pete here."

"I already have." Mirium laughed the quiet laugh of silent forests, treading lightly to them with a crumpled bill.

"Thanks," Peter said, taking it like a lump of sugar, in a tone practiced and habitual, hiding supreme embarrassment.

John scratched his rough red beard, "Stick around till I shave, will you? I'm due up at Columbia."

"Don't tell me you're teaching!"

"Just lecturing—at a godawful hour." He got up and went to the small bathroom that had no door. "How'd you make out in—where was it you were, anyway?"

"San Francisco," Peter said. "Dead."

"Don't tell me you got homesick for this crud?" John stopped for a moment in amazement then continued to shave.

"Yes, I did," Peter said. He let a pause fall. "What about you? Are you going to move? I see they're tearing down the block."

"Eventually, I guess." John reached under his chin with the razor to grate the sandpaper there.

"They're going to have to relocate you."

"Who the hell wants a new rat hole?" John boomed. "No sir, we settled for cash instead. We're buying a house on Long Island, but I'm not moving from here till the wreckers come."

Mirium had gone into the other room and now came back holding their baby, a tiny black-haired girl with John's Scottish blue eyes. She sat on the edge of the bed with her, both of them watching the two men, an archaic smile on Mirium's face, like the Assyrian sphinxes in the museum. Peter turned to play with the baby's hand—the only baby, he decided, that he liked in the whole world. It was a quiet child.

"Where are you shacking?" Mirium asked.

"Down with Elaine," Peter answered.

"How is she?" John asked with concern. "She won't tell me."

"Working on a painting," Peter shrugged.

"I thought she must be. She hasn't been out for days. Mimi's left food for her but she's refused it." John put on his clothes quickly, unable to be neat and tailored because of his large frame. His clothes hung loosely on him. "Her old girl friend's been staying with her."

"Nicole?" Peter suddenly understood the reason for the painting. "I see Elaine's had proper care."

"She's changed since last year." Mirium spoke and her quiet, high voice broke the monotony of the dark apartment.

"How do you mean?" Peter turned.

"You'll see," she shrugged. The baby was tickling her ear and she turned to peck its cheek, then pulled down her slip to expose one small round breast to its hungry mouth, modestly, aesthetic in her role of motherhood.

John was ready to go. He went over and embraced Mirium and the baby in his massive arms and kissed them both, then took his wallet from the mantelpiece and led the way out of the apartment, down the creaking, slanting stairway that no longer had a banister. His heavy steps shook the entire house. Peter followed lightly behind him, at a safe distance.

"Say," John snapped his fingers, "we could fix up the second floor for you again. It's empty."

"Won't the landlord object?"

"The wreckers are coming any day now," John dismissed it with a wave of his hand. "He won't know the difference."

Outside, the sun had come out to warm half the street and they stopped to take a deep breath. This was the only time when the smog was thinner and almost safe to breathe.

John walked with his hands in his pockets and he looked

distinguished in his only suit, his weight adding majesty rather than comedy to his appearance. No one ever dared to challenge this giant. Nine parts of his authority came from his physique, intimidating in its appearance, heavily backing up the knowledge he hammered like a spike into the heads of his students.

"I won't bring up a bunch of killers!" That was his favorite expression. It had kept him out of a high-paying job designing missiles and it had kept him out of important government grants but he shrugged stubbornly and pointed to some little boy on the street or photographed in a magazine. "See that kid? He's no genetic freak. I don't want mine to be either."

There was no talking to him about it. He had seen the figures on the atom tests first-hand, had watched the rates rise on cancer and leukemia, had anticipated the contamination of milk. He wanted no part of the arms race. Among the Washington bigwigs he was now considered an eccentric hothead—a bad security risk because of his friends. But the universities couldn't do without him. He had a mind; even if he wouldn't sign a loyalty oath, they needed him.

There was no black spot on his record—he split his vote between Republican and Democrat, he hated Communists for what they had done to the Jews and the homos and the Catholics and the intellectuals and the wealthy class—he couldn't bear the coffee shop socialists or the Bundist fascists, or the American Legion. They were all the same to him—groups trying to take over his America, trying to destroy its present mixed-up, lovable structure, goofy as it was, materialistic, unfair to all minorities, prudish. But he wouldn't sign a loyalty oath any more than he would hold a Party card. "It isn't fair to the ex's," he said when they asked him. "You can't condemn a man for a political mistake he made thirty years ago when it was fashionable to join."

And so the college presidents shut their eyes, tied a few knots in the red tape and didn't hire him on staff, but made him a lecturer, a consultant, anything else just so he could keep on teaching, keep on giving off those beautiful working theories on anti-matter, on solar power, on the magnetic structure of cells. And once in a while some liberal foundation would give him a grant. Right now, he was working on warped magnetic fields.

"Where do you intend to look first?" John spoke now, referring to Peter's job hunt.

"I thought I'd try Brentano's," Peter answered. "They might need floor men."

"Back in the book mood, I see," John grunted.

"I sure as hell don't want to wait on tables."

"Why not try something more ambitious even?" John's steps were long and spry; Peter had to run to keep up with him.

"Like what?"

"Damned if I know."

They were quiet the rest of the way—they were both silent types. John was making notes on his lecture; Peter perused the want ads on the bus.

Peter left John at Forty-second Street and began to walk up the long row of shops on Fifth Avenue, stopping to ask the Record Hunter if they needed salesmen, bypassed the banks, checked some of the men's shops, then went past Brentano's to the benches in Rockefeller Plaza.

It was a beautiful day—too lovely to spend indoors. He sniffed the potted flowers, ignoring his hay fever, and decided, as usual, that man belonged roaming the fields with a club in his hand, always slightly hungry and slightly cold, slightly hot in the groin, but not answerable to anyone—a law unto himself and his strong right arm. It would have been delightful to perish violently in such a jungle instead of this dying piece by piece, hacked away by the system of boss-employee, of status and class, of manliness and adequacy.

He had felt the yoke and the lash when very young. Out of joy in the air and the sun and the parting of spring into summer he had mowed his front lawn. He was ten. His mother smiled in approval—a jealous mother who clung to his nicely washed pink ears and flattered him in every way; a woman who did not openly wish for equality and who depended upon religion for stature in her household—any religion that took her fancy for a few weeks—setting up her own example of God's existence that could not be challenged, thus becoming the tyrant priestess of the household. He mowed the lawn and his mother smiled in approval, and it became his task from then on. He was paid for it; it became drudgery;   it was not a spontaneous labor anymore, this mowing a lawn in the sun and fresh air. It would never be spontaneous again.

His father did not have much more to offer him. In the export-import business, Peter Clausson Sr. had profited during the Depression and had paid conscience money to some of his friends who had not been as fortunate. After a while he got thinking that he was better than they were, more resourceful, shrewder. He took pride in his mechanized house—the dishwasher, the waste-disposal gadget in the sink, the television-fm-hi-fi set, the Cadillac with hydraulic bulletproof windows that he had borrowed on his soul for. And he worked long hours, and on Sundays, said little of importance and nothing enlightened, paid all the bills, doled out Peter's allowance and checked the list of chores he had had to do all week to earn it. Peter Sr. waited impatiently for his son to grow up and take over the business and insisted that Peter spend his summers bookkeeping there.

Peter had grown up in an atmosphere of convenience and economic security, without ever having enough money of his own to keep up with the expensive social activities of his high school set, always in dread of the future that sat waiting to vulture him—the two awful alternatives—the Army and the export-import business. He failed at both. Looking back this way, his life seemed like a series of failures; each more flagrant than the previous one.

2.

It was nearing ten by the clock in the store window and Peter forced himself to get up. Brentano's would be opening any minute and he walked back toward the bookshop. He had no fear of not getting a job—not here in New York where no one demanded either pedigrees or references. If there was no work at Brentano's he would find it elsewhere. He was still young and could bluff.

But time was beginning to crowd him. He knew that in one way or another this year would be the last of his life, the last year of his youth. The dark wheel of routine was his only future. He had been fed through the gears of industry; his identity was a social security number; his census report was an IBM card; he knew how to type, barely; someone had once taught him to use a dictaphone. He had been manufactured as a modern, efficient young man with automation as his only future expectation. He preferred to be a salesman or a waiter or a ditch-digger, but right now he wanted to sell books.

At Brentano's, he was lucky enough to catch one of the supervisors unlocking the door. "Do you need a floor man?"

The man smiled and shook his head. "Try the travel agency across the street."

"Thanks," Peter saluted and jaywalked across between two fuming buses.

The doors to the Meridian Travel Bureau were already open and the girl inside was typing away, electrically.

"They said across the street that you might have a job."

"Do you know travel agency work?" she replied, still typing.

"Yep," Peter lied, leaning on the counter with the self-assurance that never failed him in time of need.

"I'll have someone interview you," she sighed, shutting the machine. She got up and went into the back room.

Peter sat on the edge of the foam-rubber sofa, seeming quite efficient. He didn't mind travel agency work. The large window would let in the sun and there would be plenty of standing on his feet—he hated a sit-down job, couldn't stand fluorescent lighting. He pictured himself behind this counter, assuming a positive-thinking approach about being hired. He decided on a phony reference from an agency in San Francisco that he had once applied to. He knew a little about the work—had certainly traveled a lot.

A personable young man came out of the back office, the sort of washed-behind-the-fingernail, could-be-effeminate type who has read all about France and is dying to hit Rome as soon as he can wrangle a free trip from the airlines. He sat on the sofa next to Peter, with a broad smile, and an application form in his hand.

"I just got in from Dallas." Peter crossed his knees primly and looked intently at the interviewer with the sort of magnetic gaze that had always made him appear a man's man. "I was a partner in a small heliport there. It failed so I'm back." Secretly he laughed at the flagrant lie. "Two years ago I worked for the Thru-Ways Agency in S.F." He waited.

The young man nodded approvingly with a smile too used to being turned on for customers rather than for job applicants—a noncommittal smile with a little subservience under it and a great contempt, all at once, as if his mind had thought a hundred words or so of something that had nothing to do with the subject at hand and he had hardly listened to Peter's talk at all. "Would you fill out this application? Then I'll tell you a little bit more about the job."

He was in. Peter could feel it in his bones. There was nothing more to do but chat pleasantly.

"Could you come in tomorrow morning?" the young man said, finally.

"Perfect. I won't need much time to get settled."

Outside again, Peter enjoyed his last day of freedom. He decided to walk back to the Bowery by way of Firth Avenue. Walking helped him think better. John's words about the empty second floor were haunting him now. Even if it were only for a few weeks, he could fix it up, plug up the holes in the walls and burn coal in the fireplaces for heat, as John and Mirium were doing upstairs. At least it would be close to Elaine—would give him a chance to be with her. He wanted to get close to Elaine again, wanted to dig up the past, wanted to resurrect old ghosts. Fall had come around once more and he was ready to feel married, ready to think in terms of long winter nights, in terms of cat and wife and rocking chair.

Elaine. He would stop and buy sour cream. He loved her today, needed desperately that she love him. There could be no compromise anymore, no failure on his part to bring this about. This year he would no longer be able to turn back, would no longer be able to run from himself and from her, or from the whole godawful past.

John was another of his hopes. John stood for the educated class, a class to which Peter burningly wanted access. Long ago he had closed the doors to college himself and now he wanted to open those doors again, wanted badly to throw himself into academic life, wanted to be somebody with a degree—but now he was thirty and it wouldn't be easy. The government wouldn't pay for him. He had flunked the Army.

He had no talent for making the right friends. In the Army, that sort of weakness wasn't tolerated. He enlisted to avoid the draft at the start of the Korean War, hoping to enter college afterwards. He never left the States and spent his time idly in camp near San Francisco, doing work some WAC volunteer might have handled more easily.

There was a lot of spare time. The Commies moved in to take advantage of it. There were a lot of ex-C.P. members in the Army then—many of them in high-ranking posts, officers left over from World War II days when being a Communist was fashionable and not at all shady. But now the political tide had changed and the C.P.'s changed their stripes, some, earnestly, others, just on the outside.

One of the favorite ways to throw monkey wrenches in the war effort had been to point the finger at the wrong people. The Commies worked out an efficient system: first they entrapped the homosexuals and tried for blackmail and wherever they failed, they exposed the queer to Army Intelligence, letting the Army's axe fall on hundreds of potentially good soldiers, as well as many others who were not queer but seemed effeminate.

Then the Commies went after the other boys, not only in an effort to convert them to the Party, to get information—they had a more efficient espionage system to take care of that aspect—but to use them in their propaganda campaign, making the naïve ones into sitting ducks for Army Intelligence, gaining, with each new Army cleanup, more support from the disillusioned slobs who saw the axe wielded so unmercifully on their buddies, saw that men where being convicted on the basis of guilt by association and evidence so flimsy it would have been thrown out of a civil court.

In Peter's camp a few of the boys were too young and too clean-cut to get a real turn from the girls, too young to drink in bars, and a little too intellectual for the U.S.O. Some were queer, some, potentially pink, others, hard-shelled Republicans.

One of them had an apartment in town and so they gathered at his place once a week and drank cognac and listened to Brubeck and Thelonius Monk. They put money in the kitty to buy booze and this made it a sort of informal club. They had discussions. Sometimes they discussed politics—an important issue in a camp that might be shipped overseas to kill men they didn't know and couldn't understand. They took up Plato's *Republic* and someone compared it with Karl Marx. Some of the boys were outspoken about their beliefs, secure in their tradition of free speech. But as the axe took its toll outside, the group became more intense. A few of the members chickened out and new ones joined the crowd. The topics took up a new fervor. Some of the speakers were definitely Red. But it was hard to tell—political philosophies are never clear-cut, there was no mention of overthrow of governments.

Peter was a sitter but mostly he adored the bookshelves and the record collection and the cognac he couldn't afford to buy. He wasn't a he-man and physical labor had never appealed to him. The Army had built him up but it hadn't made him like dog work, or the Army. He hoped he could sit out his term without being sent up front. He didn't like the idea of killing or being killed. Living in a barracks with a bunch of guys of varying I.Q.'s had already disrupted his sense of inner comfort—he had always cherished privacy, had always had a contempt for shower-room comparisons, for bedtime jokes, for food cooked in grease and for master sergeants with bad diction. Perhaps that had been the reason that Intelligence had picked on him. They knew he could be easily cracked. Perhaps that had been the reason they had worked on him to tell on the others.

Peter shut the hot lights out of his mind.

Now he supposed that they had really gone easy on him, that they had gone easy on all the others who weren't really to blame. But that hadn't been the point—he could forgive them for his undesirable discharge but not for making him a coward, an informer. When they made him a coward they had taken away his life. He could no longer respect himself and so, to himself, he, Peter Clausson, had died.

Peter reached Twenty-sixth Street now and decided to cut east through the park, thinking the thoughts he always thought when he crossed this park which had rails on each side of the walk so that people could more efficiently be kept off the grass. That had been the sum total of his life—that a rail had always been between him and the cool green grass.

After the Army, he had to return home, suddenly, inexplicably, back into his mother's eager arms. His father did not dare ask shy he had come back so soon for fear he might discover, in his son, a weakness—psychological, perhaps, or physical—some slight imperfection that he himself could not face because, after all, the failing might have been passed on to Peter by one of the hundreds of ancestors among which Peter Sr. was numbered.

And Peter gave no excuse, brooded for weeks, then suddenly threw himself into night college and into his father's firm with the intensity of a sinner seeking punishment. The result was a D average in school and a mess of costly errors for the firm. He had begun to destroy himself. Everything he did pushed him further toward that goal. Then, in another wild moment, he packed a suitcase and left home.

At twenty-two, he found himself in the Village, waiting on tables in a dive—one of those notorious after-hours places that always risked a vice raid, even though they paid much protection. Compulsively, despite his intense dislike of dirt, he wiped the tables and felt himself whole for the first time.

He remembered now that the entertainer had been progressive, high on tea and with skin black as velvet—a tall primitive with a civilized mind who looked like the trunk of a tree when she sang to music low and quiet like the wind. The customers were a mixed crowd, as in most Village clubs; some lesbians, some tourists, some junkies and a couple of plainclothes cops on a night off.

Peter had successfully avoided making friends among the regulars, content only in his new-found self and in making his small furnished room into a home. The waiter's job paid good money—over a hundred a week, mostly in tips with no tax to report. For a while, his bank account had helped him forget college. Medical school had refused him because of age and there wasn't any point to studying science—not with his security rating. Teaching was also out in the same breath. That left the administrative sector—useful for his father's business. To Peter, waiting on tables seemed a more welcome future.

"Hey! Boy! *Garçon!*" The holler came from the rowdy crowd in back that had no respect for the music and was followed by jeers and laughter. Although it wasn't Peter's station he want back to take the order just to shut them up.

"What'll you have?" He took out his check pad to write on it.

The waiters never noticed the customers and the customers seldom noticed the waiters. The man was halfway through the order before they happened to look at each other for a moment. The reaction was delayed thirty seconds and then the fellow got up and crashed his table over to the floor.

"Why it's you—you yellow rat!" He stood there, tensed in a drunken rage, seeming ready to pounce. "I knew I'd find you sometime!"

Peter remembered him vaguely. He had slept in the same barracks with David Kranz for a while. He had been one of the pros, the bunch that re-enlisted every three years—a rough, tough guy with more brawn than brains, who had his stripes reduced three times for brawling. Seeing him now left Peter too surprised to react. But the guy was doing enough reacting for both of them.

"This queer ratted on my buddy," he said to the group. "He's a lousy, filthy pigeon!" He was the sort of man who had only two tones of voice—one was a boisterous shout and the other was a whining rage. He spoke in his whining tone right now, his whole red, freckled face twisted—a leather face with weathered grooves in it, the kind of face that inspired fear or alarm in his opponents because it was always belligerent.

"Sit down, please," Peter said with a calm that surprised him. Still, he was puny by comparison—Peter was nearly a foot shorter.

"Sit down hell!" Kranz spat out, stinking of spilt beer on his clothes. "I'm going to beat you up!" With the slow movements of a drunk he began to clench his fists.

Peter steeled himself for what would happen. He had never been in a real fight before and he dreaded the though of being in one now—dreaded hurting someone else as much as risking being hurt himself. The group was obviously a bunch of servicemen in civilian clothes, probably just back from overseas. They were a dangerous crowd, had been heckling the singer for an hour and had made it hell for the two lesbians dancing on the floor. They were all high on boiler-makers.

"*Yessir* I'm going to fix you good," Kranz threatened. He picked up a nearby bottle of beer and smashed it on the side of the fallen table.

Peter knew it was hopeless to stay and fight him. Despite his boot camp training he knew himself to be out-muscled and outsized, yet he could not get up enough fear to run away —as if he was merely an impartial observer and the man wasn't really after him.

He knew why he felt that way, knew he felt impartial because he didn't feel alive any more, had lost all respect for himself—but, too, he was burning with a quiet anger, a stubborn need to fight back. This need made him stay, quietly waiting for Kranz's attack, even though he was painfully aware of the cruel weapon in the other man's hand. Instinctively, he grabbed a chair and held it out as he might to a tiger, while people cleared out of his way.

"What's the matter? Yellow?" A cruel smile formed on Krantz's face.

"Come on and find out," Peter said, his eyes fixed on his opponent's eyes—beady, animal eyes, waiting for an opening, waiting to leap.

"I'm gonna show everybody what a yellow rat you are," Krantz taunted.

They sparred for a moment, each waiting for an opening, a stumble, a hasty move. They were in the back room of the bar where bloody fights were allowed to go on, uninterrupted by the manager or the bouncer as long as the furniture wasn't wrecked. There was no help expected, no one would come to break it up if it got too rough. Peter knew the danger. The broken beer bottle, tight in the drunk's hand, baited him menacingly. He lunged for it, using the chair as a shield, hoping to entangle the man's arm.

Krantz grabbed a leg of the chair with his left hand and pushed it back, entangling Peter. The chair came out of Peter's hands and clattered to one side.

Now Kranz lunged, an evil leer on his face, and Peter saw the glint of an upraised broken bottle just in time to avoid its vicious, ragged edge. As Kranz staggered by him, momentarily off balance, Peter let some deep, primeval instinct twirl him around and he found his right fist traveling with surprising power into the beer-belly of his opponent. It landed. A beer-impregnated belch escaped the drunk, its stench assailing Peter's nostrils. Taking advantage of the bully's surprise, Peter quickly followed with a solid left to the nose. Blood spurted onto Krantz's shirt front. Enraged, he wiped away the blood with one mighty paw, then rushed at Peter like a crazed bull, swinging the raw-edged weapon downward at Peter's throat, missing each time as Peter side-stepped, then coming down again and again, the weapon just barely missing each time.

Peter now found an aspect of himself that frightened him. It was actually sheer pleasure to fight, sheer pleasure to outwit his opponent, to feel the great demands put upon his welterweight frame. Suddenly, he was filled with a need to win, not because of the horror of the broken bottle—he knew a sickening fear every time it whistled past his cheek—but because of the fight itself, the awful pleasure of it and the need to continue, to aggress, to finish what had started—with victory or death.

Kranz came at him again, blood coloring a red bib under his chin, the stink of his sweaty body strong in the room, his eyes shot with drunken hate. The bottle descended once more. Peter side-stepped again but this time a raw edge of the bottle grazed his cheek and he tasted his own blood salt on his lip. Keeping a wary eye on the bottle he whirled and threw another lucky punch at Kranz's already injured nose, causing a new fountain of blood to spurt.

"I'll kill you for this!" Kranz bellowed, and mouthing obscenities, he cast the bottle aside and with it all his caution. He charged Peter anew, his long, solid arms flailing and forcing Peter from an offensive to a defensive position. One arm struck the top of Peter's head and Kranz's other ham-like fist descended with pile-driving force on Peter's shoulder. A kick to the shins followed, rapidly succeeded by a sharp right to Peter's chin. Now Kranz moved in for the kill. Peter found himself completely enclosed in a vise-like, beer-stinking, sweat-reeking hug. The drunk spread his legs for a more solid foothold and squeezed, squeezed, squeezed . . .

Peter's vision blurred, his chest seemed to cave in, his lungs starved for air. He gathered all his remaining strength to keep from being crushed by a deadlock that seemed frozen in time. The superior size and strength of his opponent had won out and Peter felt himself slipping, sliding down a long chute, the blur changing from gray to dark blue, to deep, pitch-black, ebony darkness . . .

From a great distance—was it the same world?—Peter heard a new challenger. "Sit down and listen to the music, sonny," the disembodied voice rumbled, as though from the bottom of a deep well.

Peter felt a sudden release—a rush of fetid air seared his throat, his windpipe leaping and gulping at the stunning influx. Nearer now, he heard Kranz snarling, "Okay, fat boy, I've got enough left for two like you."

Through the blur in his eyes Peter could make out the shadow of John moving in on Kranz with almost jovial authority, unafraid, completely sure of himself.

"Let's make this one quick," Kranz leered and his fist shot out at John's middle, a fat, inviting target, the obvious but foolish point of attack. The fat man stood his ground, barely flinching at the force of the blow, deftly grabbing Kranz's wrist with his left hand as it reached his belly, then quickly brought his right hand in to assist and twisted. Kranz's arm was turned almost completely around and his body turning with it, convulsed with pain, straining against the massive strength of the giant.

There was a loud snap, like the crack of a whip, and John released his hold. Without another glance at Kranz, he turned to Peter. "You'd better leave with me, boy," he said.

The crowd went back to their tables—order quickly restored. Only Kranz stood, in the middle of the floor, his face mirroring disbelief, his arm hanging limply and uselessly by his side.

Still bleary-eyed, Peter wiped the sweat off his face and straightened his clothes. In as few words as possible, he explained to the deadpan manager. His job was gone. He couldn't work here any more. Someone might come back to find him someday. The word would be passed around.

Out on the hot August street, they formally introduced themselves and John made a joke of the whole thing. But Peter felt he had to tell him the story. He hadn't told it to anyone else.

"You don't have to explain it to me, boy," John interrupted him. "I know the treatment they give you."

It brought the past vividly into Peter's mind—the overly-neat and handsome captain, precise in his manners, stating the facts with quiet sadism: "If you don't sign this you'll face court martial. You could get up to twenty years."

"I'll bet they gave you the old one," John continued, "about protecting a bunch of Reds and queers."

Peter nodded. "In a way they were right. There were one or two Commies in the crowd."

"Of course they were right," John interjected, raising his voice. "You did the only right thing."

Peter looked up at him, surprised. He hadn't expected John to say that.

"They had to root out the informers," John went on. "There wasn't any easier way."

"But the other guys—"

"It's just too bad about the other guys," John interjected again "Every war has casualties, more than just the ones up front. The weak are always the first to go, keeping the rest of the crowd strong, and mean." John said this sadly and with an inner rage that made him pant and walk faster in the hot night.

Peter thought about this. Yes, the war had killed him. He had died for Korea no less gloriously than the GI's who got it in the field. Might he have been one of those if they had sent him up front? He would never know, and yet he knew he had never wanted to die, wasn't the sort to willingly sacrifice his life for any abstract cause. It had taken him years to learn to love his country—in the Army he had still been too young to form a set of values. It hadn't been Intelligence that was really at fault but the whole world, for sending regiments of its surplus children to slaughter under the theory that peace and freedom, justice and plenty could only be won by the sword.

That had been seven years ago—that night he had met John. So many things had happened since then. John had been a beat-bohemian scientist living on the top floor of the little tenement that was always on the verge of being torn down. Elaine had come to the basement two years ago, when Peter was living on the second floor. . .

Elaine. He had reached the Bowery now and was a block away from home. He remembered hunger and stopped at the grocery store to buy sour cream and baby food for her and lentils and sausages for himself. John's five was going a long way. He still had two dollars left. It would suffice until pay day.

He carried the bag of groceries to the house and kicked in the basement door. Elaine was still naked and asleep. He put the groceries down by the bed and sat on it, watching her. The room was stale with turpentine—no bedbugs or roaches would live down here—even so she smelled of the woods and meadows, a white Venus untouched by crud.

He longed to put his hand on her flesh. It had been an awfully long time. He wondered if he might kiss her and then bent down to brush his lips on her breast. It tickled and made her turn toward him in her sleep. He could no longer resist taking her lips and pressed his mouth on hers, ever so gently.

She responded automatically and he pressed the rest of his body against hers, feeling her exquisite nakedness through his clothing. His hand went down to her thigh and caused a spasm of desire in her, waking her from her coma. Her eyes opened and saw him and for a moment it seemed as though she wanted him—but only for a moment. Then, with a look of great unhappiness, she turned her face away from him. He didn't want to force her. He sat up again and sighed, "Now I feel I'm really home."

"Please go away, Peter," she said. She was crying.

He obeyed, taking off his jacket and starting to tackle the heartless task of cleaning her kitchen. He was compulsive about dirt, especially now when it gave him something else to do than talk to her. He wasn't ready to talk to her. He didn't know how to begin. All he could think of was how he wanted her. That was what had been wrong last year—they had never conversed, just copulated.

He began to clear the floor of debris—symbolically, as if he were doing that with his life. He disposed of the garbage first, turning his nose the other way, and squished the maggots underneath. That made him feel a little better. The rest would be easier. He had just gotten around to cleaning the sink when Nicole of the painting opened the door. She was startled and then recognized him.

"Oh, it's you," she said in a French accent. She was a tall girl, almost Peter's height, well curved and Greek-nosed, cute enough for Hollywood and much too feminine to be butch. But Peter knew she was butch, or, as the French pronounce it, *bouche*. They had met once before, momentarily, two years ago in this basement. Now she held a large bag of groceries she had brought with her and carried it to the refrigerator, stuffing as much as possible on the top shelf.

"I'm glad Elaine's been getting the best of care." Peter leaned on the sink to watch her. He was being sarcastic on purpose.

"You are no one to talk," Nicole countered. "How awful you were!"

"Oh? Elaine talks about me?" He smiled, interested.

"Sometimes." Nicole finished with the groceries and went to remove her sweater. Peter appraised her. She wasn't ugly like the painting. But Elaine had caught the awful intensity in her eyes. He typed her as an *enfant terrible*—not more than twenty-one.

"Elaine." Nicole now went to sit by her bed with a look of great concern. "Wake up. You must eat."

"I'm not hungry," Elaine mumbled.

"Look what I have for you." Nicole unwrapped an expensive quarter-pound of smoked lox, ready to stuff it into Elaine's mouth.

"Hey, don't do that." Peter rushed to her and grabbed the package away from her.

"Give it back!" Nicole shouted at him. "She has not eaten in two days."

"That's nothing new," he said, taking a slice and eating it himself. "Do you know smoked fish could kill her?"

"What do you mean?" Nicole's voice was high but the accent made it pleasant, despite her excited tone.

"Go heat some of the baby food in that bag," Peter pointed with authority. "Go on—or don't you know anything about ulcers?" He took another slice of lox and then went back to the sink.

"Ulcers?" Nicole understood him suddenly. "Of course." She did as he said and went to the stove with a jar of Junior Beef Stew from Peter's grocery bag. Peter handed her a just-washed pot.

Between the two of them, preparing Elaine's meal took a short time. When the jar was warm, not hot, Peter poured the contents into a bowl, got out a container of sour cream, two antacid pills from the bottle on the dresser, and went over to Elaine, waving the stew under her nose. Elaine's lips and nostrils twitched and she opened her mouth wide to let Peter feed her. Nicole watched the process with great fascination.

"She's too hungry to wake up," Peter explained.

"Should I pour her a glass of milk?" Nicole said, hovering.

"The soure cream's better," Peter said. "Her stomach's shrunk. We'll have to feed her slowly." He patiently held up spoonful after spoonful and then, suddenly, Elaine opened her eyes and tried to sit up. Peter fixed the pillow behind her so that she could raise her head.

"Elaine, it's Nicole." Nicole knelt by her side with urgency. "It's my day to pose."

"Oh, yes," Elaine mumbled and tried to get up. The mention of her work drove her, compulsively, despite the pain in all her muscles.

"Lie down," Peter commanded. "Do you want to throw it all up again?" He handed her the rest of the sour cream and the beef stew so that she could feed herself. Elaine started to protest but then saw that Peter was right—it was wiser to rest awhile.

Peter stretched and then went back to cleaning up. "You might help me with this mess," he said to Nicole, cruelly calling her away from Elaine's side.

"You leave all that alone." Elaine was too weak to shout. Her voice was a hoarse whisper.

"I'm just dusting," Peter said and continued with his tasks. From the corner of his eye he saw Nicole kiss Elaine's hand but decided not to make a scene. Instead, he took out his anger on a dozen dirty plates and then moved the furniture a little so he could sweep. There wasn't much he could do. A year of dirt had encrusted everything. It would be better if he started fresh with the second floor, making a decent place for them to live until they tore the building down, leaving the downstairs just as her workshop—as it once had been, last year.

The noon siren wailed and he stopped spreading the dust with the worn-out broom. He went to the laundry hamper for his old pair of jeans and found them too dirty to wear. He decided to spend a dollar on laundry. He filled a couple of pillowcases with sheets and shirts and towels and then took Elaine's sheets from under her, leaving her completely naked.

"Peter's here so I'm supposed to be clean again," Elaine sighed patiently to Nicole.

Peter kissed her again, impudently, and this time she didn't fight him. She was remembering for a moment. Nicole impatiently tapped her foot. Peter stopped and helped Elaine to sit up. She had regained her strength and now reached for her jeans but he snatched them from her. "It's the wash for them, too."

"Oh, no," she moaned. She didn't want to be naked now. It was cold.

Peter went to his suitcase and sacrificed a shirt and a pair of shorts and tossed them to her. Then he picked up the pillowcases and left the apartment, bringing them to the laundromat up the block. He felt good. The cobwebs were clearing today. Elaine would come back to him. Today was a clean, new beginning.

3.

When Peter returned from the laundromat he went directly to the second floor and paused to reconstruct the memory of how it had once looked. A Puerto Rican family had moved in and had left again since last fall and the place was now in great disrepair from the forced overcrowding of poverty. He would have to wait until pay day to really do a good job on it—such items as Lysol, bleach, masking tape could not be bought for fifty cents. Today all he could do was sweep and throw out the garbage that had mysteriously accumulated even up here.

Years ago, John had helped him make the second floor into a castle, dated 2000 A.D. (Atomic Detonation). John's inventive genius had gone wild constructing an electronic nightmare. Peter's kitchen had been a science fiction writer's dream—with a clock radio that set off the rotobroiler, a robot device that broke an egg and dropped it on a pan, a burner that turned itself on and made coffee, and an arm that reached around Peter with an electric razor as he tossed in bed, waking up leisurely. There was also a stereo set—before they came out on the market—with four loudspeakers that reverberated for blocks in all directions. Electric eyes burglarproofed all his windows and a transistorized air conditioning set de-ionized the air he breathed, making the smog more tolerable.

The same sort of equipment was in John's apartment but that was always in somewhat of a mess because John could never be neat. The two had spent winters in hermitage working at their hobby and combining it with John's more serious experiments, which sometimes threatened to set off a minor atomic blast.

For John, Peter's friendship had become a joy. The fat man had always been lonely, a misfit among the rest of his colleagues because of his age. He had been a brain child—one of those who got doctorates before twenty—and other physicists were always out to discredit him. There wasn't any place for him in the world of science before thirty; no one wanted a precocious boy, they were too unstable. He belonged teaching at Princeton but Einstein had been still alive then, and John was too fat for the Army.

John had spent his wild youth in coffee shops and bars, glaring at the crop of girl bohemians who flocked in from all parts of the country to go to college and to live in the Village. He had sat mostly in the Rienzi on MacDougal Street—where *Life* sometimes took pictures of him—strangely clad like all the others, with blue beret, embroidered shirt and a tyrolean jacket. John liked to masquerade and seemed somehow gracious in his outfit, despite his weight, almost not ridiculous. He had since grown out of this stage—the one he had been in when he first met Mirium.

She had been a medical student going to N.Y.U. They, the college students, all seemed to live at the Rienzi, left their bundles there between trips to other stores and coffee shops and bars, carried on a huge and almost instantaneous communication system via the bulletin board there, rented a favorite table around the clock for the price of a cup of coffee. Mirium sat there in the afternoons, between two and three, often alone, her nose deep in *The Fundamentals of Pathology*, calmly munching on some tidbit as she turned page after page with diagram after diagram of gory dissections and cross-sections. John had glanced discreetly over her shoulder. "May I buy you a cup of coffee?"

Mirium had looked up, surprised. She wasn't a pretty girl. She had been, even then, scrawny and awful-looking in clothes, and she seldom was approached except by the usual creeps who will approach just any girl at all. John might have been one of those and she might have reacted quite differently, except that John already had a reputation in the Rienzi, and everyone knew who he was. For this reason, perhaps, she was friendly. "No, please, don't spend your money," she answered, smiling. "But do bring your cup over, if you like."

John was floored. It was the first time something like this had ever happened to him. He took his cup over as if he were hypnotized and sat and waited for her to say the first word.

There was a certain grace and tenderness about John and Mirium's romance—the romance of the homely. Each had been through the stage of seeking only outward beauty in a partner, in a feverish attempt to make themselves outwardly beautiful by association. The beautiful had cruelly rejected both of them, putting the mirror up to their faces and saying, "Look at how ugly you are. I can't possibly be attracted to you." With the mirror came the realization of their own homeliness that nearly destroyed both of them with pain. But they were both intelligent as well as sensitive and from that pain was born a vast and indomitable compassion for the rest of suffering humanity, and their eyes began to see new things, began to see the beauty of minds instead of bodies, of ideas instead of appearances.

"She likes me!" John had said to Peter, coming home giddy that night, as if a truck had winged him.

"Who likes you?" Peter had asked. It had been a long time since John had met a girl—a girl who was interested in him. It was 2 a.m. and they sat in Peter's apartment, waiting for the robot to wheel over the coffee.

The master-mind looked dumbly at him. "She kissed me. She had to stand on the park bench to do it but she kissed me."

"Who are you talking about?" Peter repeated.

"Mirium . . ." John sat and tried to recover from the experience. A week later, they were married.

The change that Mirium wrought in John was miraculous. He matured, gave up most of his bohemianisms, took to wearing clothes that were not ridiculous, stopped trying things like hashish and peyote, stopped going to bars and sitting in coffee shops, even began to think seriously about making money and insuring their future, tempered his hotheadedness so that it did not interfere with his productivity or job opportunities.

The change John wrought in Mirium was almost as spectacular. She became beautiful all of a sudden, no longer plain, gaining the sort of charm that Cleopatra may have had, despite the ugly long nose depicted on gold coins. Mirium didn't stop going to school, and was still a medical student now, but she gained a new assurance about her ability to accomplish difficult feats—a sort of masculinity in the way she approached her subjects that was very different from the shy, apologetic ways she had always won her A's. But in all other things she was still Mirium, quietly efficient, friendly but retiring, solicitous over John and a sort of handmaiden for him when they were together, catering to his tastes and idiosyncracies with the patience of a saint. Upstairs, even now, they lived in constant bliss.

Peter's turning point had come not much later. It had come two years ago when Elaine rented the basement.

The basement had once been neat and livable—long, long ago. So had the second floor. Peter looked at the filth that had piled up in a year's time and realized that he had to go downstairs again to borrow the broom and the mop. Later, when John came home, they would put in the furniture that was now stored upstairs at John's and downstairs, at Elaine's. Perhaps everything could look almost as it had looked last fall. The thought filled him with energy and he ran nimbly down again and crashed through Elaine's door.

"Came down for the broom," he announced.

Elaine threw a sneaker at him. "Get out of my hair."

She was trying to make some sense out of the havoc he had wrought among her paints. Nicole was in the chair they used for posing, her blouse off, fidgeting with the corner of a sheet that would not quite cover her luscious bosom.

"Whoops, pardon me," he said facetiously, and put one hand over his eyes. He groped for the broom and the mop and left in a hurry.

He knew he was being cute. He might at least have knocked instead of barging in on what easily might have been a tender love scene—but he hadn't wanted to be tactful. Now he felt slapped down. Nothing improper had been going on downstairs at all. And yet it was impossible to believe that Elaine had been faithful to him all year. He had no right to ask it of her—after walking out as he had. But she still loved him—at least that was plain, plain in the way she had responded earlier to his kiss and plain in the way she had just thrown the sneaker.

Elaine loved him with the same vehement hate she had always felt for him. She had always needed to love him with hate—it was the only way she dared to love. She was an angry young woman. Everything Elaine did always seemed to lead to self-destruction. A Massachusetts debutante from the Northern Baptist belt, she immersed herself in filth to purify herself, to separate herself from the sinful roots of the wealthy religious set—not at all the proper ancestry for a young American Existentialist. Now, in 1960, she was called, much against her wishes, a member of the Beat Generation. But Elaine wasn't beat, she was whipped—self-flagellated like Saint Francis. And, for the lack of time and strength, she now fasted in crud, although she had once cared so much about cleanliness.

When Elaine had come to the basement, she had been a pale-blond Garbo without lipstick, her hair knotted primly behind her like a schoolteacher's. She wore jeans rebelliously and did most of her own moving in, picking up great boxes of books from Nicole's station wagon. She and Nicole had labored like convicts for a week, painting and sweeping and making the basement into what it had never been before. It had been well worth their effort—the rent was only twenty a month.

Peter had watched their progress with interest, feeling too shy to say hello. But he was dying to meet them, especially Elaine, and longed to borrow a rare edition of Henry Miller's *Miscellanea* which he had seen resting on top of the pile of the last carton of books.

John and Mirium had also watched the two and were pleased to be getting such compatible new neighbors. They wouldn't object to the hi-fi playing at all hours. And when it became obvious that Elaine was moving in alone and that Nicole was just a friend helping her move, all of their hopes to include her in their social life had grown more intense.

"Why don't you just knock at her door with your *Four Saints In Three Acts* album and make an exchange loan?" John had suggested, trying to push Peter into making the first friendly gestures.

"I don't think she likes men," Peter shook his head.

"The hell with that, boy! She's all alone now," John had exclaimed, "so try your luck anyway."

Peter didn't like the advice. He loathed making himself a nuisance where he might not be wanted. But after a while he talked himself into it. He put on his white flannel trousers and took his album of Gertrude Stein and bravely knocked on her door.

"Hello. I live upstairs," he said self-consciously.

Elaine had opened the door only a little and looked at him like a frightened deer. "Come in," she said in a gesture of hospitality so deeply ingrained that she would not have been able to shut out anyone, even a rapist, if he had greeted her politely.

Peter studied the basement. It was spotlessly neat and full of color from the many shades of material that covered the bed, the chairs, and the windows. It was poorly furnished but that fact went unnoticed.

"I wanted to let you know the whole building's full of egg-heads," he said awkwardly.

"I know," she smiled distantly and turned back into the apartment, full of poise now, no longer startled. "Would you like coffee?"

"No, thanks, I don't want to impose." He stood, hesitant, clutching the record album. "I see you live alone now."

Elaine seemed puzzled for a moment and then smiled. "Oh. Nicole just helped me move."

Involuntarily, Peter sighed with relief. "I just came down to offer a loan of my record collection in exchange for a loan of some of your library." He waited.

The same weird smile formed on her sensitive lips, almost as if she were laughing at him. "I don't have a phonograph."

He decided to be more forward. "In that case, perhaps you'd like to come upstairs and hear some stereo tapes. I have a pot of coffee on right now." He paused, watching the strange smile come again, making him feel almost angry at her distance from the scene. But then she spoke, shrugging. "I guess it's all right." She went lazily to the bookshelf, moving from the thigh like some thin and graceful panther. "Which one did you want?"

"The Henry Miller," he said quickly.

She bent down and found the small volume on the bottom shelf, then straightened and wavered for a moment, the world suddenly spinning before her eyes, and she put her hand out for balance.

"Are you all right?" He reached over to steady her.

"Yes, quite." She regained herself and suddenly stepped quickly across the room and led the way out of the apartment.

Upstairs, Peter shouted for John and Mirium to come down and join them, afraid to be completely alone with Elaine—afraid of her coldness and cruel smile and her very graceful thighs that exasperated his sight when he watched her walk or sit with her legs folded Buddha-like in the chair. He turned on the tape recorder for her, putting on some of Dick Maxfield's electronic music. It was way out—just her type of sound. She immediately relaxed and threw her head back to listen to it. Her beautiful mouth—the most expressive feature of her face—curved into another sort of smile and yet, still a distant smile.

Now the coffee maker buzzed and Peter pressed a button on the control panel of his easy chair which caused the robot—a squat little monster constructed from one of those Gilbert science sets to which had been added John's rare mechanical genius—the robot to wheel a tray of cups and saucers to the middle of the room.

"Do you take cream?" Peter asked, expecting her to be startled out of her distant mood, at least to admire the machine.

"Yes, lots, please," she said.

"Say when," Peter said, pouring. She did not say *when* and he stopped when it seemed quite light, then placed the cup back on the tray and directed the caddy to wheel it to her.

She looked down when the robot stopped beside her and finally noticed it, giving a small and not-too-startled "Oh." Then she laughed a little. "I see the outside world is becoming civilized."

"Just mechanized," he smiled, glad to have evoked some show of interest on her part for her present environment.

"Are they selling these at Woolworth's or something?" she asked, pouring even more cream into her cup from the saucer that was on the robot's tray. Then she stopped. "I'm sorry. Am I making a hog of myself? I have an ulcer, you see."

"Oh." He suddenly understood. "No, by all means, take all you want. There's lots more. Shall I get you a glass of milk?"

"No, that won't be necessary," she smiled. It was a smile directed at him this time, not a faraway one. "Or did you make this one? Are you a scientist?"

Peter shook his head. "John's the scientist." He looked toward the hall now, wondering what was keeping John and Mirium. Apparently, they were taking their time on purpose.

"I think it's charming," she said, patting the caddy on the head as if it were a dog. But she was aloof about it. She had not yet completely lost her distant manner.

"It's still no substitute for real people," Peter said, a little sadly.

She drank her cup of coffee and then filled the cup with more cream, clutching her chest as if something uncomfortable were happening there. "Do you have a problem about being alone too much?" she asked, forcing the question out between sips.

"Yes, I tend to have," he nodded, observing her with great interest. Her face was ghostly pale, much whiter than it had seemed in the red glow of the basement, where all the colorful upholstery had cast a wholesome light on her complexion. He noticed that the whites of her eyes were stark, as in cases of extreme anemia, and that the blue of her pupils had a doll's eye look, tense and glass-like, light like morning skies, fathomless and yet fragile—easily whitened out of its own color by a change in the reflection of light around the room. He suddenly became very concerned for her but did not have time to ask if he might be of help because then John and Mirium entered in a burst of enthusiastic noise.

"Sorry to take so long, Pete," John boomed. "Well, so this is our new neighbor. Welcome! Welcome!" He went to shake Elaine's hand vigorously but then sensed that she was not strong enough to accept so hearty a greeting. He merely patted her hand. "I hope you won't mind our neighborly ways. We're rather proud of our little intellectual outpost in this great big bedbug trap they call The Bowery." He lingered, holding her hand awhile longer. "I'm John and this is my wife, Mirium."

Mirium said hello to Elaine, beaming from behind John's great frame.

"Thank you," was all that Elaine said.

John let go of her hand and sat in his favorite large easy chair and Mirium sat on the floor at his feet, resting her head gracefully on John's left knee.

Peter sent the robot over to them and they poured out cups of coffee. The electronic music had become quite agitated and filled the room now, and they all sat back to let the mood sink in. Elaine was the first to break the mood, clutching her abdomen again and grimacing in a sardonic smile, then taking another furtive sip from her cup.

She seemed to be undergoing some awful torture and yet trying to turn the gnawing pain into pleasure, to bear it gracefully. Then her cup suddenly dropped from her lap to the floor and she gave a muffled gasp, sinking down into her chair murmuring, "How beautiful." Her eyes were beady, open rather than closed, staring into space.

"The music?" John bent forward, thinking that she meant to begin a conversation.

"No," she managed to mouth the words dryly, "the sunrise."

It made Peter almost drop his cup, realizing suddenly that something was very wrong with her stare.

"Where is it?" John stood and came near to her, to hear her better, trying to click into her train of thought.

She tried to motion to the wall. "It's all purple," she whispered hoarsely, then fainted.

John caught her hand and felt for her pulse. Peter stood over him and Mirium tried to get past them to the patient.

"She said she had an ulcer," Peter said.

John grunted, allowing Mirium room. Efficiently, as though she already had her degree, Mirium opened Elaine's eyes and felt her pulse again. "Hunger's made her faint," she announced. "I'm sure of it. I'd say she's schizophrenic—probably hasn't eaten all week."

"What should we do?" Peter fretted helplessly while Mirium and John examined Elaine's arms for possible hypodermic scars—Elaine might also have been on heroin or morphine—then, finding none, John stood and waited for Mirium to give him specific orders.

"Shouldn't we call an ambulance?" Peter said.

"She probably loathes hospitals," John mused. "No, I think it's better if we try to revive her first. Do you have any smelling salts?"

Peter ran out to buy them and when he returned he found Elaine already coming to without them, called back to life by the magical savor of Mirium's warm chicken soup which had been waved in front of her nose. They made her eat slowly, afraid of the food's effect on her stomach, and they took the bowl away after a few spoonfuls. But it had been enough to revive her. With a weak spurt of alarm she tried to sit up. Mirium restrained her.

"You'd better rest awhile," she said softly.

"I'm sorry—" Elaine made an effort to explain, having much guilt on her face, then had to lie back again and close her eyes. Mirium returned the spoon of broth to her lips and Elaine took another mouthful, hungrily, like a baby bird.

Meanwhile, John cocooned her in the chair with one of Peter's blankets, then put his hand around the back of her head, massaging away the pain that encircled it. "Have you been taking any medicine?" He paused to let her answer but she only opened her eyes again and stared at the light. "You can tell us," he tried again. "You're save here."

"I'll be all right," she mouthed, then her body straightened in a spasm of pain and she fainted again.

"We'd better call an ambulance," Mirium sighed. John got up solemnly and went to the telephone.

They all knew they were betraying her. Elaine might have slept it off if left to suffer alone, but then, she just might not have recovered by herself. By visiting them upstairs she had become their responsibility, and they couldn't take a chance on her not recovering from whatever it was—mental or physical. Her condition was serious.

Twenty minutes later, an intern and an attendant came and took her away on a stretcher. Peter felt he had to go with her and lied about their being engaged. They let him ride in the ambulance and he held Elaine's hand, hoping that she would not wake up just yet because then he would have to explain the awful thing they had done to her—would have to tell her that she was in an ambulance, on her way to a hospital.

Elaine looked angelic, Raphaelish, her head resting on the white pillow, with her blond hair in thick snake strands spread over the whiteness, illuminating her face like a halo. He thought about that and traced the sensuous line of her pale lips with his fingers. He hadn't looked at a girl since high school—since Doris. The smell of rancid hair remover filled his nostrils again for a moment, mixed with the odor of cheap adolescent perfume. Elaine wore no make-up; she wasn't at all like Doris . . .

Peter had given up on women because they seldom washed—or, at least, it had seemed that way to him—their powder was too thick and mixed with greasy creams and the blond streaks in their hair came off on his hand as he stroked it. He had needed sex at seventeen and they had teased him, had subjected him to their ridiculous flirtations, their obnoxious grooming fads, with no intention of keeping a vaguely worded promise. It had always come to the same sort of end and perhaps Doris symbolized it most acutely: a memory of a bare pair of legs stinking of hair remover, sharp with the bristles of half-grown fuzz. Those bare legs were never to lie near his own; oh, yes, he might lift the skirt if he put out the light first, but he might not ever lie between them in a way that might please him as well as her.

Yet, Doris had been a little better than most of the other available girls. Peter had dated her because she was more intelligent. Her hair was a dyed topaz and had black roots, giving it a dirty look. She was majoring in English and wanted to become a teacher, or get married. Her father owned a liquor store and this put her in the wealthier half of the class, and yet she came from lower-class stock and had much of the whore about her, in the way that she spoke and in her taste in clothes.

Peter impressed her by spending a lot of money when he took her out and then discussing worldly subjects such as politics, the arts, and Thomas Wolfe—instead of the common party topic, sex. He let many weeks go by before he even tried to kiss her—he didn't like kissing her, anyway—that was not why he was taking her out. He couldn't see kissing a girl unless he really loved her—having sex, yes, but not kissing—kissing was a show of affection he could not muster up for Doris.

He waited a few months until his parents were away one weekend, then took her out and then took her home. They had gotten high on martinis down at the Town and Country Lodge, where all the seniors went dancing when they had a spare ten or twenty and they had run into Sol and his date, a girl from some other school, and Doris had waved her arm excitedly up in the air for them to join their *tete-a-tete*. She was on her second very-dry-with-onion and the straps of her evening dress were slightly disarranged from her nervous activity. "Hey, come on over, yes, I mean you two," she had called.

Sol took his date over—a shy, starry-eyed virgin who had a Sunday-morning-at-church look in her face—that is, well groomed and proper and awkward in high heels, unused to alcohol and bearing up with her best manners, not more than sixteen.

"Hi, Pete. Hi, Doris," Sol had said, and winked at Doris. He was a dark boy, well tanned, fastest on the track team but not quite a man in looks, still without the trace of a beard and dressed in his best black suit which looked foreign to him, unfitted. Peter knew him fairly well. They had shared a table in Chem and Sol had often borrowed his notes, being suddenly panicked, helpless in the face of so much to learn and memorize. They had exchanged small talk, and at one time it looked as though they might become good friends, but somehow other people came along and there wasn't time. "Say, are you sure we won't be spoiling something?" he had said then, reluctant to join them.

"Hell, we're not lovers," Doris had answered before Peter could speak. "Sit down. Where have you been all this time?"

"Oh, around," Sol had answered, a bit flustered.

Peter called the waiter and they ordered more drinks. He was a little impatient—not mad, just bored. Doris was making a fool of herself, obviously chasing Sol right in front of him. He didn't care if the show was for Sol or to make him jealous, to make him more attentive. He couldn't feel either jealous or attentive—he couldn't care less about what she was doing. The evening and the martinis were sitting in his stomach, and he longed to take her home so he could raid the icebox—the sandwiches served here were too expensive, and Doris would be sure to order lobster or steak or something way above his means.

The band began to play and Doris tapped her foot to the corny music and finally said to Sol, "Let's dance." Sol reluctantly stood up and obliged.

Peter was left with Gloria, Sol's date, and the two watched the exhibition on the floor—a combination of belly rub and stumble as the two bodies fought each other to dance properly.

Doris laughed several times, loudly, saying: "Oh, Sol, you're a scream!" But Sol wasn't making any jokes. There was a desperate quality about her inebriation, about her voice and her movements, and Sol's manner was all self-conscious, all embarrassment.

"I guess she's a little high," Peter apologized to Gloria, and Gloria smiled broad-mindedly. When they got back, Peter stood and announced firmly that he was taking Doris home.

"See you again," Sol waved, but to Peter.

Peter drove Doris to his house for a nightcap and cold chicken. She staggered in, almost indecently, in her low-cut dress. One of the straps had broken now, and she had mumbled all the way about how silly he was to be jealous of Sol, how selfish he had been to want to leave so soon. As she spoke she undressed herself, pulling off her heavy earrings and the rest of her jewelry and then, inside, on the carpet, kicked off her shoes and straightened her girdle through her dress, not caring if he saw her. Next, she peeled off her long white gloves and stood there staring at him.

Peter realized suddenly that he would not have to be subtle, that Doris knew what he wanted and was just mad enough to play along—mad at Sol, perhaps. He went to where she stood and took her in his arms, pressing her large-boned, slightly fleshy body to him. It was like touching a blob of cold cream and his mouth searched for the only clean-smelling part of her—her bare freckled shoulder. He kissed her there, evoking a gasp, and she held more tightly to him, hung on to him with her arms around his neck. "Ooh, Peter," she breathed, and pressed her pelvis to his, locking their bodies for a moment in what seemed like a close, tantalizing dance.

He swayed her to the couch and she lay back in it, her eyes narrowed in a relaxed, dreamy way and a silly smile on her mouth that betrayed a tense expectation. Peter sat beside her and put his hand on her breast, feeling the softness there through her clothes. She moaned, but almost insincerely, and shifted her body in what appeared to be delight. Then he boldly took her hand and placed it o him. She giggled and pushed him away half-heartedly. He tried to pull down the strap of her gown to expose a breast. "No, don't," she said, "not with the light on."

He obliged, reaching up to turn off the single lamp near the couch, and they lay together in the dark, with only the light outside the window casting shadows in the room.

He had not spoken all this time—silent with lusting her too much. Now, he still had nothing to say. He patiently labored with her clothes, unzipping the back of her dress so that it would come down in front, and loosening her stockings from her girdle so that he could bring his hand to touch her. She gasped again, this time a real gasp, and he burned to take her.

"No, not there," she said, in a voice suddenly small and young.

It fazed him. He lay between her legs aching to go on but forcing himself to wait. "Are you a virgin?" he asked, whispering it in the dark room and letting the question hang tensely.

"What's it to you?" she said, trying to push him away slightly. He wouldn't let her. "Please be good, Peter," she said. Her voice was nervous but low, bedlike.

"What do you want?" Peter asked in an effort, a very patient effort to be cooperative.

"Don't ask such questions." Doris brought her hungry mouth up suddenly and he kissed her again, with all of him, feeling the hardness of her pelvis pressed against him, so hard it hurt. Again he tried to lift her dress, feeling all of her ready for him, feeling her hot breath moistening his ear and her entire soft body struggling to meet his in a throbbing expectation. But he barely touched her there when she screamed, "No, please, don't go on. Let go. Let go!" She pounded against his chest and then began to cry.

He stopped; he let go of her and sat there in a dark fighting rage, wrestling with an urge to do what he wanted anyway, no matter what she said. Then he turned on the light.

Doris looked at him. Her innocent stare added insult to injury. Peter stood and straightened his tie. "Come on," he said blankly, "I'll take you home."

"I want another drink," she said, shaken, sitting up sullenly and fixing her strap.

"Don't you think you've had enough?" he said. He was mad, not so much at Doris but at the whole goddamn middle-class world.

"Pete, don't be angry," Doris pleaded almost pitifully. She had dried her tears with her wrist and her mascara had streaked her cheeks with brown. She was nervously trying to clothe herself again, suddenly feeling half naked in the stark light.

"Why shouldn't I be?" Peter retorted. "You're nothing but a tease."

"And what do you think you are?" she answered, suddenly flaring. "Why'd you bring me here in the first place?"

"For the same reason, I guess." He had to admit it. He forced himself not to be angry and went to pour both of them a fresh drink. She hobbled over to him as he did so, lifting her arm. "Be good and zip me up, will you?" She sounded sexy again. He turned from the drinks to do so and she said thank you cutely and stood on her toes to peck him on the lips. Suddenly he slapped her, hard but not hard enough, before he even realized he had wanted to. He saw her cry and hold her cheek and it relieved him to have hurt her.

"I hate you," she said, deeply wounded.

"I hate you," he returned, then regretted it. He felt sorry for her but the harm was done. She took up her stockings, still holding her cheek, and went to the john.

When he took her home it was all forgotten. "Do I see you tomorrow?" Doris asked at her door, a certain apology in her voice.

"No," he said.

"No?" She looked at him, hurt for a moment, then shrugged carelessly as she entered her house. "I should worry. Good night." Her words were suspended in the air but Peter didn't answer. He stepped on the gas pedal and drove off.

It was mostly his pride that had been hurt, because he realized that she had done this before, with others. The sharp edge of the knife came a week later when he ran into Sol again. Sol called Doris a whore and said she had let him in. Peter decided that it was probably a lie, but the lie cut deep anyway—the thought that Doris would let Sol but refuse Peter. So Peter lied to Sol in return. It was the thing to do—to lie about getting further with a girl than was actually the case. It wasn't that Peter said it bluntly but rather, he refused to discuss the matter with Sol, insinuating that more had gone on than was proper to report.

Through high school, he had preferred his pillow to girls like Doris and later, preferred it to the fare at the local henhouse. Finally, the Army cured him of his manhood.

He was still under-aged when he was stationed in San Francisco—that had shut him out of the decent bars. The indecent bars had girls in them but who wanted them? Peter especially didn't want them but for an even stronger reason: he had been assigned to the reception desk in the infirmary, where he was graphically exposed to the nature of V.D., seeing slow-witted privates sometimes coming in too late, their organs half eroded by the ravages of social disease.

Then the Army had discharged him as an undesirable—that had proved he hadn't been man enough to stand up and fight with the others. They made him an informer and cured him of courage. Then, manhood and courage gone, they proceeded to label him queer because, of course, what else could he be—a lot of his friends were. This mark on his record would keep him from ever becoming a teacher, from ever holding a decent job—would subject him to persecution from every local policeman who cared to look up his past. Yes, the Army had killed him, but he was still alive . . .

Elaine was still alive, too, rocked to and fro as the ambulance turned a corner. Her head moved slightly and her eyes opened. Peter took hold of her hand. "You're all right. We're taking you to a hospital."

She would have been startled but his tight hold of her hand kept the world stable. She sighed and closed her eyes again.

Peter continued to hold her hand, feeling the smoothness of her thin white fingers and suddenly wishing very hard that he might become her friend, might penetrate the barrier of her eternal preoccupation and enter her inner circle of acquaintances—the people who were able to speak to her and get a reply.

He stayed only long enough to see her admitted without difficulty and to find out the time of visiting, then walked home.

4.

Peter had been an insurance salesman when he first met Elaine and his time had been his own so that he was able to stop in at the hospital during the early afternoon, between calls. On his first visit he brought her a few paperbacks and some pink carnations. Against her cheeks, the flowers made her look ghostly white. She accepted them meekly, not quite able to get up and feeling rather trapped and out of place in the world. "See if you can get them to close the curtains?" she pleaded with him. Those were her first words. He didn't bother to ask the nurse's permission and pulled them around the bed himself, making hers a private room. It brought gratitude to her pale face.

"Have they found out what's wrong?" he asked, sitting in the low chair by the bed.

"I keep telling them it's my ulcer but they're putting me through diagnostics anyway," she said sardonically. Her voice was not a whisper but it was barely audible, having no strength to it.

"Some intern needs the practice." He tried to sound cheerful.

It amused her. "What's your name again?" she asked.

"Peter Clausson," he said. "You're Elaine Perkins—I saw it on your mailbox."

"Hello, Peter," she smiled.

Suddenly he knew that she had accepted his presence in her life. It elated him, filled him with conversation. "Is there anything I can bring you from home?" he volunteered. "I can come back tonight with it."

She nodded. "My keys are in my jeans pocket. Ask the nurse to get them, will you?"

He got up and went to find the nurse—a dried-up little old lady with short red hair. She sighed wearily when he relayed Elaine's request, opened the curtains without saying a word, and old him she would bring them as soon as she had time. He went back to Elaine's bedside, closing the curtains one more time. Elaine then asked for his pen and some paper and began to write down a list.

He watched her write and suddenly wondered how he ever could have thought her cold and distant. Her mind was alive now, aware of everything around her—not purple-sunnish at all as it had been the night before but full of wit, mixed with a desperate impatience to leave this place, to be free again.

The head nurse broke the spell of the moment, coming with Elaine's keys and finding the curtains drawn. With a hostile determination, she pulled them back again.

"Please, I want them closed," Elaine protested with her best effort.

"Nonsense. The air has to circulate," the nurse dismissed her complaint. "You're right by the window—you can't keep all the fresh air to yourself." She put the keys on the table and walked away.

"I'll go mad if they're not closed," Elaine shouted weakly after her.

Peter immediately got up and closed them again, only to find that the nurse persistently returned to open them one more time. "It's against the rules to close the curtains," she said and walked off.

Elaine picked up a pitcher and was about to throw it at her in a sudden burst of angry strength, but Peter caught her in time. "They'll have you in the psycho ward if you do that," he said. He eased her back on her pillow. "Relax. I'll speak to the doctor."

Meantime, her outburst had evoked three self-righteous smirks on the faces of the women patients in the beds across from her—housewife types who enjoyed gossiping more than reading. The curtains were quite an issue by now, Elaine's having complained about them all morning. One openly commented: "Why shoud you have more privacy than the rest of us?" Another insinuated that something had been going on behind those curtains.

Peter turned and gave them his best vehement stare, then left Elaine to find an intern.

It was not a trite complaint—having the curtains drawn meant the world to Elaine. She could not bear to be a part of an assembly line, had to feel apart from the crowd, had to have her privacy because it was closely connected to her entire identity, to her feeling of existence. Peter understood, felt the same way, and suddenly he realized that he loved her, loved her because he felt every bit the same as she did about the curtains.

But his pleading with the doctor made no difference. The head nurse was boss on those matters; the curtains would have to remain open.

He went back to tell Elaine of his defeat, phrasing an oath that he would get her out of there as soon as possible—but it wasn't as simple as that. Her ulcer was in a serious condition, the outburst with the nurse had made it bleed again and he returned to find her vomiting a pint of blood. The staff took over then, drawing the curtains shut, and it was requested that he leave the scene.

Obstinately, he returned that night with the things she had asked him to bring and, finding her under heavy sedation, merely left them for her and went away again.

Her condition didn't change for a week. He consoled himself by defrosting her refrigerator and feeding her cat—a skeleton of an animal with a sweet disposition. John and Mirium came down to help him and they finished painting her bathroom for her (she had barely started one wall the day of the purple sun) and washed the dishes and dusted. Helping Elaine had become an interesting pastime for them, making them feel the wonderful sensation of being good neighbors, as in small towns.

It was John who first dared to look at her paintings, taking them out of the corner where they had been stacked, their faces to the wall. "They're good," he said. "I wish I knew an art collector."

When the hospital finally allowed Elaine to have visitors again, Peter showed up bright and early with a bunch of lilacs and snapdragons. He found the ward in a commotion and Elaine happily drawing away with the pad and crayons he had left for her.

"Glad to see you've adjusted," he joked.

"It's the rest of the ward that's not doing so well," she chuckled in reply, then proudly showed him what she had been drawing. It was the picture of one of the women across from her, except that in the drawing she was nude and on a bed pan. "She's in for a *d-and-c*," Elaine pointed and whispered loudly. "That's polite for abortion."

Peter looked at Elaine. She was bursting with vicious good health. Her cheeks were slightly pink and her blond hair glittered in the sunlight that came through the window. "If they're going to make a stink about my privacy I'm not going to let them have theirs," she said, putting the finishing stroke on the drawing and then setting it up so that it could be seen by all. It was alongside two others she had already done.

Peter looked at them with mixed emotions, trying to hold back a smile. It embarrassed him to see them but they gave him a wonderful feeling of victory. Elaine had clashed with her environment and had come out on top. Now he noticed that the rest of the ward was discussing the issue rather hotly and that the head nurse was being summoned.

"I'm only drawing the busybodies," Elaine assured him, starting on another sketch. "Stick around and watch the action."

Elaine was almost in a maniacal state, working very quickly with her pencil. "Id' like to introduce Mrs. Larkin," she said, not stopping her feverish drawing. She gestured to a very old lady lying in a bad condition in the bed next to her. "Mrs. Larkin, this is Peter Clausson," she said in a respectful tone, but not stopping her work. The old woman looked up at Peter and half- nodded. He noticed that both her hands were bandaged for no reason and that the bandages were tied to the bed post as if she were a prisoner. Before he could puzzle it out, Elaine asked him if he had a pocketknife.

Peter obediently searched for one in his pocket and then came up with his key chain that had a small blade on it.

"Would you lend it to Mrs. Larkin?" Elaine asked. Peter hesitated, puzzled. "It's all right," Elaine assured him. "She's been trying to untie those bandages all day—they're so she won't pull out her catheter." Peter looked at the old woman, obviously half-senile, who gestured as excitedly as she could at the sight of the knife, smiling eagerly. "Please, Peter," Elaine pleaded. "How would you like being tied up like a dog just because someone's too prissy about getting the sheets wet?"

"Yes, the knife," the old woman labored, still gesturing.

On an impulse he felt must certainly be wrong, Peter handed it to her and watched the old lady eagerly cut the strands. She returned the knife gratefully to him then reached eagerly under the sheet to remove the painful contraption which obviously had not been properly vaselined.

The head nurse arrived just then with perfect timing and stood there sputtering, not knowing what to say first. But Elaine was ready for her. "Go away before I throw up my tranquilizer," she said with a stone face.

It stopped the nurse dead in her white shoes. She must have suddenly realized that Elaine's chard said "NO EXCITEMENT." With a frustrated gesture, she closed the curtain. It brought a victorious hooray from both of them and Peter spontaneously embraced her.

"Sit down. I'll draw you," Elaine said.

She did a sketch of him as he watched her hands move surely on the pad. She was getting well and her fighting back at people had helped her. He didn't know it then but it had been the first time that she had ever fought back except through her own world.

Elaine had to stay another week before the hospital reluctantly let her go—at her own risk. They gave her a mess of prescriptions and explicit directions about what to eat and what not to eat and begged that she visit their clinic at least once a week. The hospital bill went to the City because she didn't have a job and said that her parents were dead. That had been a lie. They were living up in Massachusetts but she didn't want them on her neck.

Peter came to pick her up and took her home in a taxi. She was strangely quiet, accepting all his solicitude without comment. He wondered what she thought of him and whether the word for it might be *chump*, but it really didn't matter what she thought of him—he couldn't help wanting to do everything for her.

When they reached the house Peter paid the fare and took her things down for her, then helped her carefully down the basement stairs as if she were pregnant. They were standing in her apartment and he pushed the door shut to keep the street grime out. He didn't want to leave yet, wanted to welcome her in some way and to assure her of his help. She observed him silently for a moment, then removed her coat, not waiting for his help.

"I wish I had something to offer you," she said finally, embarrassment in her eyes.

"John and I stoked your cupboard," Peter smiled. "Shall I warm you some milk and make me some coffee?"

"Thanks," she said, stupefied. "Well, sure, I guess."

He went to the stove and filled the pot Mirium had supplied.

Elaine felt weak in the knees and lay down on the studio couch. She had lost a lot of blood. She watched Peter as an invalid might watch a nurse, with a tired resignation to her illness and a little feeling of discomfort at having to be idle.

Then John and Mirium invaded the basement, peeking first through the small window and then daring to open the unlocked door.

"Hullo. May we invite ourselves in?" John said.

"Yes, please," Elaine said, sitting up a little, eager to see them. "Peter's making coffee."

Peter came into the main room again, bringing Elaine's glass of milk, and she thanked him with an affectionate look in her eyes, her mouth forming the words as if they were pearls. It made Peter flush.

"How did they treat you at the hospital?" John asked, starting the conversation.

"Fair," she said good-naturedly, "but let's forget it. Peter tells me you're a scientist."

Mirium laughed. "John's making an atom bomb upstairs. Haven't you heard?"

"Yes, that's the latest," John said eagerly. "I haven't even told you, Pete. It's a tiny thing, like a toy—no more than an inch long. I'm working on trying to explode it in a controlled chamber—so maybe we won't have to use the atolls to try out the big ones. When it's perfected, I'm going to mail it to the President—disarmed, of course." He sat back and chuckled.

"Are you serious?" Elaine asked. "I think it's a wonderful idea!"

"They're ribbing you," Peter said. "You'll have to get used to their practical jokes. John only works on peacetime projects."

"You'll have to get used to me, too," Elaine blushed, looking down.

"I'm very gullible."

Peter served the coffee then and they assumed a festive mood, the party taking up where it had left off two weeks before. Elaine struck up a beautiful conversation with John on abstract values and Simone DeBeauvoir's *Ethics of Ambiguity* which brought out, piecemeal and reluctantly, Elaine's rigid Baptist background and her strong feelings of rebellion against it. John's forbears were Catholic but his conclusions were the same as hers—"There's altogether too much telling people what they cannot do."

"But one shouldn't permit crime," Mirium interjected between chess moves in a game she had started with Peter.

"Too many things are lumped under the general category of crime," John answered her hotly—he always discussed things hotly.

"Like that ulcer diet the doctors gave me," Elaine took his side, "a whole long list of things not to eat and a small, vague list of things I'm supposed to have. It should have been the other way around."

"Quiet! I'm almost in check," Peter said, closing his ears. No one stopped talking. He had given up trying to compete in the conversation. It was impossible to impress Elaine while John was around—that was like trying to compete with Einstein. Instead, he had started the chess game with Mirium—quiet Mirium who seldom spoke above a murmur, except to argue with John. And now, in the same stupefying manner that she accomplished everything she set out to do, Mirium timidly moved her queen and Peter's king was hopelessly checkmated. He scratched his head, wondering how she had done it.

"Finished?" John looked up instantly, having followed all their moves while talking to Elaine.

"I surrender," Peter said, putting his hands up.

"Good!" John got up and stretched. "Time to go, Mimi," he yawned, then stopped Peter from getting up, too. "No, don't break up the party. Stay awhile and see if Elaine wants a few things done—more milk, maybe." He winked at Peter.

Peter shifted, not wanting to seem forward. He had contempt for the Don Juan approach since his time with Doris. It might have been better if he wooed Elaine for a few years first—she was so delicate and untouchable.   Then Elaine decided the issue, calling out suddenly, "Yes, stay awhile, Peter—if you want to."

Her voice struck him like warm sunlight.   "All right," he shrugged.

He accompanied John and Mirium to the door, then closed it behind them and walked to the center of the room again, sitting on the edge of the straight chair.   It made him seem quite unrelaxed.

"You don't talk when John's around, do you?" Elaine smiled partly because of his distance from her, but it wasn't a seductive smile.   It was, rather, the same removed purple-sun smile he had seen that first evening.

"He says things better than I do," Peter answered.

Again she smiled.   "You haven't any ego.   Where did it go?"

"It died years ago."   He relaxed a little and dared to look at her. "Tell me about the purple sun.   Do you see it often on walls?"

She was puzzled for a moment and then remembered the incident. "Yes, quite often.   I live in a purple world most of the time."   She was partly joking but in a bitter way.   "The saints got that way, too, you know—all that fasting."

"I know," he nodded.   He decided that he couldn't stand the distance between them and boldly went to sit on the floor near her bed. "Are there people in your world?   Men, I mean?"

"No," she said, pausing, seeming to want to qualify her answer.   But instead of doing so she sat forward and measured the distance between his nose and eyes and ears with her fingers.   "I know what I did wrong in that sketch," she said spontaneously.   "Do you want to hand me that pad?"   She motioned to where it lay beyond her reach on the art table.

He got it for her but instead of passing it he impulsively took her hand.   His face was very near hers and John had mentally slapped him on the back—*Go on and kiss her, boy.   Don't give her a chance to argue.*

Peter had not wanted to kiss Doris but now he ached to kiss Elaine. He reached up and took her mouth with his, expecting some sort of miracle to take place when their lips touched.   But it was like kissing a statue.   She did not draw away and so he pressed his mouth closer to hers, longing for some response.   There was none.   Her passive resistance began to embarrass him and he was left sitting quite awkwardly on the floor, his hand still by her cheek, searching her eyes for some show of emotion. Her glance was distant. "Shall I leave?" he asked cautiously.

"No, stay," she said, preoccupied. He tried to kiss her again but she pulled away and placed her cool hand to his lips. "But don't do that." Again her voice was absent. "Please hand me the pad."

He handed it to her, suddenly understanding. She had something else on her mind and couldn't stop to listen to him until she had finished what she wanted to do.

He watched her ketch quickly, sensuously, getting down lines without pausing to erase wrong ones, getting at the essence of what she saw in his face, substituting new impressions for old. "You don't smoke, do you? No, you have nice white teeth," she said finally, still drawing. "I like men who don't smoke—my Baptist upbringing, I guess. Can't stand men who smell of tobacco."

"Sometimes I drink," Peter smiled, posing quite still.

"So do I," she said wryly, "but my ulcer's on the wagon."

"What about sex?" he ventured.

"Occasionally," she answered, without giving the question importance. "Don't talk now. I'm drawing your mouth."

There was something sexual about the way she wanted to get him all down on paper. At least, her entire body burned with a feverish excitement that made even the muscles of her legs tense and aware of his physical presence. The most extreme pleasure was concentrated in her hands and eyes as they worked together to accomplish the drawing—to possess him on paper. She was not passive in this act—she was the aggressor.

"I'm glad you're not asking me to take off my clothes," he commented as soon as her crayon had moved away from the lower part of his face.

She laughed slightly. "That's not necessary. You see, it's not you I'm drawing—it's the light as it bounces off your face, all the different shades of it, the grays and the lighter grays. I'll never get it quite right but I've got to keep on trying to put it all down."

"Why?" he asked, mostly to keep the bond of conversation.

"Why?" She paused for a moment and then resumed more fervently than before. "Because after some bomb blows up this whole crazy world, some digging anthropologist a few million years from now might come across this piece of paper—charred, faded—and he'll be able to offer it up as proof that at some approximate time I lived, and you were there to pose for me." She stopped. The drawing was finished. Without bothering to show it to him she closed the pad again and put it on the floor.

"Shall I go or do you want more milk?" he asked, getting up to stretch.

She gave an ambiguous and preoccupied no.

"No to which?" he asked.

"No to both," she answered, coming back to the present. "I'd like some Junior Beef Stew and sour cream."

"Mixed or separate?" he asked.

"Just throw one over the other and stick in a straw," she sighed, slightly disgusted, then lay down on the bed to rest. She was wearing the jeans she had worn on the night they took her to the hospital. Her feet were bare and she shivered slightly. He saw it and brought over a blanket.

"Why are you so good to me?" she asked, her eyes half closed.

"I'm hoping you'll throw me a pearl," he said. There was a slight cynicism in his voice. He was convinced now that she could never be interested in him except as a model. And yet he couldn't help letting himself be used by her. She needed him and had no one else to care for her. However, his words had made an impression on her. She spoke almost as if drifting to sleep. "Peter, please be patient with me. You don't know all I'm fighting."

It made him remember for a moment how very ill she had been the last two weeks and how preposterous it was for him to hope that she might now be full of desire for him, just because he had kissed her. She was too sick to play Juliet.

He warmed the beef stew and put the sour cream on a separate dish, topping it with Junior Plums and Tapioca with Apples, then brought the two bowls over to her bed and began to spoon her the stew. She accepted the food lifelessly for a while and then noticed the dessert and gave a delighted squeal, waking again and immediately beginning to eat faster to get to the sweets.

He watched her. She was little-girlish when she ate. He longed to kiss her cheek softly where her blond hair stopped beside her ear, longed to make her delighted over something more than food. Again he wondered whether he might dare to try to hold her again. He forced himself to wait until she had finished and had set her bowls aside, then he sat on the bed beside her and took her cold hands in his, warming them. "I guess I'd better say good night now," he said, exercising great self-control.

It made her laugh a little and he could tell that she was laughing at him rather than at some other private joke. He straightened with indignation, getting up to go.

She saw it and said, still with amusement, "No, please sit down. Stay." She motioned with her hand, patting the place on the bed where he had just sat. He sighed and humored her, quite impatient but not terribly angry—more disgruntled than angry.

She ran a finger gently up his arm saying, "You're being very patient and sweet."

"It's a role I'm not used to playing," he said, trying to make himself out to be more severe than he though he could be. He wasn't rreally severe at all, had never been able to be. Elaine saw through him and smiled her distant smile.

"What's so funny?" he asked, annoyed.

"You are," she said. "You have your own purple sun to contend with and you don't even know it."

"What do you mean?" She had placed him on the defensive.

"I've watched you in your other world all evening." She paused and traced the veins on the back of his hand playfully. "You're not very used to other people either."

"What makes you think that?" Peter coughed. She knew too much about him—had divined too much.

"Because you're so compulsively kind, yet your eyes are always wandering. But I can't help being fond of you. You're the first *gentle* man I've met who isn't busy spouting platitudes." Her strong words pierced his private world and he turned his eyes toward hers for a moment. Hers were clear and blue and unblinking. "I do want you to stay awhile," she added sweetly.

He knew then that he might kiss her now and that she would pay attention to him, not to some other thought. He took her mouth again, thirstily, not trying to hold himself back, and embraced her with his body, falling on hers so that they lay full length on the bed.

Her body reacted violently to his, finding warmth in him to take away the chill in her bones. "Oh, yes, Peter," she breathed when he let go of her mouth, then kissed him bitingly, bringing her body forward so that her legs locked around his and all of her cradled him in an embrace that had more strength in it than he had expected of her.

He was not prepared for such a strong response—had not dared hope for it. The surprise paralyzed him for a moment and suspended everything, until she impatiently took his hand and brought it to the buttons of her jeans.

He obeyed her unspoken request and unfastened them, discovering with a shiver of pleasure that she wore no underwear. He felt her soft flesh press toward his hand and he caressed her thigh, making her moan softly.

Her head lay back on the pillow and her body was quiet for a moment, her lips slightly parted as if she were about to speak, but her hands spoke for her, coming up slowly to his ribs and resting lazily on his belt. she unbuckled it meticulously and found the bareness of his stomach with her cold, bloodless fingers. Then her hands became warm and he found himself caressed, befriended for the first time by a woman, held prisoner in a tenderness that confounded his lust.

He let her continue, wanting to come into her and yet unwilling to defile her. He had seen her angelic face—that same distant smile had formed on her lips, pure of carnal things. He hesitated and she waited and suddenly he realized that nothing could defile Elaine—that now she was no different from a moment ago, when they had been conversing—realized that Elaine would always be the same because she was herself in all things. With this realization, all need for urgent decision left him and he quietly undid the buttons of her blouse as if he were undressing a small child. But it exposed her white breasts and they were not a child's. He lay his head between them and her hands left his groin and held him in an embrace as her whole being waited for him to take her.

He filled her body with one strong thrust of uncontrollable passion and saw her wince with pain.

"I'm all right," she said, "go on."

But he could not go on. The moment had been short, shorter than he could possibly have imagined and he was grief-stricken over his inadequacy. As for Elaine, she clung to him, reconciling herself slowly to the knowledge that she should not have expected to be pleased. He covered her nakedness with his body, trying to make her warm, and then asked feebly, "How do you feel?"

"Like a whore," she said, staring at the blank wall, "but it's all right. It'll pass."

"It filled him with guilt and his guilt made him bitter. "Do you always feel that way?"

"You're the only man I've slept with," she answered, not looking at him, her eyes fixed to the wall.

That had not occurred to him. She had not behaved as he might have expected a virgin to behave. But he had no reason to doubt her because she had no reason to lie. Elaine was too generally disinterested to care what he thought of her.

"Would you believe me if I said you were the only woman?" He spoke to her in the same toneless voice and then watched doubt come into her eyes.

"Not with *anyone* else?" she asked, incredulous.

"Awful, isn't it?" he smiled. "But it's true. I've always lacked the patience to play at preliminaries. Was it that way with you?"

"No," she shook her head and turned again, "you're just the first man. But there were others." She let the cryptic answer hang and he wondered if he might ask her what she meant. Who were the others? He remembered the girl who had helped her move into the basement—Nicole. He remembered what he had thought about them that first day, seeing them in bluejeans, aloof and withdrawn and ivy-leaguish—he had thought they were lesbians then. But he had since denied that to himself, wishing with all his heart that Elaine was not.

"For me there were no others, men or women," he finally replied.

He expected his statement to evoke some sort of admission on her part but instead she smiled wryly, "Well, bully for you!"

She sat up, naked but not self-conscious about it, took one of the blankets for a toga and went to the john . . .

5.

"But there were others." Her own words rang in Elaine's ears as she desperately fought the feeling of Peter. She hung over the sink in the john and unwillingly met her face in the mirror. It was not a changed face, just much in pain—the pain of the ulcer revived all over again and making her world red. She would have to go out again but right now a door separated her from Peter.

"But there were others." How loudly that resounded. There had been Nicole, and there had been Phyllis, back during Barnard days when they shared an apartment, and now Peter—the shock of Peter.

Why was he so different, so foreign by comparison, like touching the hard bark of a tree after caressing soft velvet? Her flesh now stung and bled from a thousand imaginary scratches. It was his sweat on her skin, burningly foreign, and his odor in her nostrils, foul after the perfume of Phyllis and Nicole.

Phyllis—that had been the mistake. They had been roommates, both studying for the ministry and anxious to sacrifice themselves on the altar of foreign missions where leprosy and malaria waited to greet them among the thousands of starving, withered bodies who lacked the consolation of faith in God and the Beyond, where all was supposed to be bliss.

Phyllis had been a strange, repressed girl, younger than Elaine and full of uncontrollable moods that led to self-exhaustion in all she undertook—led to her setting up impossible goals in studies and in friendship. Elaine had watched her silently as Phyllis fought with herself—the self she could not face—only to bounce back from all four walls of her private prison. She was a homely girl with curly blond hair and large bones that gave her a horsey appearance; but for Elaine, Phyllis was beautiful to draw: the triangles of her figure made graceful patterns when put on paper, primitive, archaic. Elaine had sat quietly and drawn her as Phyllis struggled to cram, struggled to think clearly despite the cloud constantly blocking her concentration.

This went on for months and one day Elaine had come home unexpectedly. She smelled gas escaping underneath her door. When she entered the apartment she found Phyllis, nearly unconscious, with her head in the oven. Elaine shut the burners and quickly opened the windows, then returned to make Phyllis breathe air again. There was no need to call an ambulance; the whole matter was better kept between them. When Phyllis revived she broke into sobs and clung to Elaine, cursing herself for what Elaine finally gathered—after decoding her disjointed sentences—had been an all-consuming passion for Elaine.

Schoolgirl passions, to be expected from a sheltered nineteen-year-old. But the revelation pierced Elaine's aloof, introverted world. The thought of making love to Phyllis, of making love to anyone, male or female, was foreign to her entire being. Elaine had given up passion when she gave up the erotic dreams of adolescence in one of those self-mechanisms that shut out all thought that one cannot morally accept. Elaine had sublimated in some way—had transferred all her drives to some sort of saintly dedication to the spirit of life, grandiose and loving in the way dawns came up every morning and green grass smelled wet with dew. Now that spirit of life was also in her arms, in the form of Phyllis hiccupping with sobs—homely, intense Phyllis.

Elaine put Phyllis to bed and then paced until twilight, standing by the window with the view of the Hudson River all orange in the setting sun. Phyllis' confession had awakened a desire—not so much physical as spiritual—a spiritual need to be of use, to do something of consequence, to communicate a form of love. It was not passion. Elaine could not feel passion, not for anything but all of life itself.

She walked over to Phyllis who now slept with the exhausted sleep of seraphim after a bout with Milton's Satan. Softly, she woke her with a touch of her hand. Phyllis clutched her hand and met Elaine's eyes with a look of fervor, pure, innocent fervor that waited for something to happen that she did not even know how to express in words.

Elaine could not bear that look. She brought her lips to Phyllis' open mouth and transformed her entire being into an instrument of fulfillment. Their bodies wrestled, not to repulse but to combine, innocent in all knowledge of love-making, aware only of a need to pass through each other, to defy the law that two cannot exist in the space of one. Their breasts, their pelvises were locked, their arms and legs knotted and their mouths met and let go in the search for a kiss to end all other kisses . . . And at the end, failure, because neither knew how and each was afraid to learn.

Phyllis married soon after. Eventually Elaine had met Nicole, but that had been a completely different matter. Elaine told herself that a feeling of power had been her only pleasure in women—power that made her see things through the eyes of a man, that heightened her perception of the bouncing sunbeams and made her understand all living things as God might.

That same feeling of power had been in the appeal of the ministry and her wish for power had made her choose Barnard, a a step or two from Columbia's theological seminary. Elaine would have made a magnificent preacher. But she had stopped believing in God. Not because of Phyllis—it all had to do with Blake's *Tiger.* It was not true about the divine concern for sparrows and lambs if vultures existed to pick on the live bowels of wounded deer and if half of the race of Man was still inhuman.

Elaine had delved into the accounts of witch trials where heretics, dismembered of hands and feet, were thrown alive on burning coals; she had watched the apathy of the congregation ten years after Dachau as they continued in their petty bias against Jews; she had observed ants as they consumed a struggling worm and had seen maggots festering on the back of a grazing cow.

Elaine had always had a private war with God. It was not a war against existence, however—rather, a change of emphasis from concern for God to concern for Man. She wanted to wipe out the inhuman race—but in a human way, not by mass murder. Thus far, the opposite forces were gaining ground: the inhumans were getting set on all four corners of the earth for a mass demolition. These were not different races or followers of different creeds, not Mongolian or Teutonic hordes. Now the whole species was too interbred for that excuse. No, somewhere back in history a race of robots had mated with a few *Marlboro* smokers to produce a general effect of violent genes versus gentle ones: one soft baby to three with hearts of steel.

Elaine was still certain that Peter had been one of the soft babies. When he first came into her life she had thought so. She had watched him struggle to make up to her for the awfulness of the hospital ward. She had coped with it herself but it had been good to have him there in league with her.

She had never rebelled so openly since grammar school when she drew Michelangelo's David absent fig leaf to upset her teacher. It had broken up the entire class, as her sketches had disrupted the hospital ward. Both times she had gotten a wonderful sense of relief at doing something so outwardly rebellious and this time Peter had been her partner in crime.

She had wanted to repay him for his kindness and solicitude, but she had not expected him to fall in love—love was a not a responsibility she had wanted to be burdened with again and yet—there was Peter, a new millstone around her heart . . .

"I love you," he said. It came spontaneously, as she returned from the john. She refused to take it seriously.

"Don't be silly," she answered, coming back to bed.

The words slapped him and she noticed that he was hurt. "You hardly know me. I'm dull, selfish, frigid."

Peter kissed her hand. She knew he wanted her again and she steeled herself to go through with it one more time. After the softness of a women she had not expected his hard male body to be so coarse and rude by comparison. Now it took a tremendous effort on her part to keep from snapping at him; her nerves were raw.

"What's the matter?" he asked.

It made her start, afraid for a moment that he had guessed her mood. "Nothing," she said. Then, as a stroke of luck, her ulcer began to gnaw. "I guess I need more food," she added.

Patiently, he got up to wait on her. She watched him playing housewife in the kitchen and it touched her. She should not disillusion him simply because she had a mess of problems. She determined to be less selfish.

When he came back he found her sitting up and smiling. "Leave the food for a while," she said seductively. He left the food on the coffee table and sat on the bed again, made curious by the look in her eyes.

Peter caressed her and Elaine tried to think of Nicole, arguing to herself that surely there could not be that much difference between her and Peter. She closed her eyes and tried to pretend that it was all the same—but it wasn't. . . .

Elaine had met Nicole shortly after she had changed her major from philosophy of religion to art history. Nicole was a model—the sort of model who takes off all her clothes and poses with complete abandon and then wraps herself up doubly well in a bulky, all enfolding bathrobe.

Nicole did not have to model—her family was wealthy and her father was an American engineer—but she wanted her own pocket money and, most of all, wanted to feel free of the middle-class conventionality that pervaded her home. She was a beautiful girl, built like an Italian street urchin—muscular and straight—with breasts carried high and yet round enough to form a graceful profile.

It was after the life session was over that Elaine really noticed her, when Nicole wore the bulky bathrobe. Elaine had put the finishing touches on the nude without a face that she had been sketching—the nude with Nicole's body, but it was only a manikin, not really human except on paper, completely detached from the girl who now rubbed her tired legs, wrapped in the bulky bathrobe, feeling herself watched. Elaine looked up from the sketch and their eyes met.

"May I see it?" Nicole asked, in her Parisian accent.

Elaine patiently opened the pad again and exposed the drawing.

"It's good!" Nicole said. "How could you do it so fast? It is the best I have seen of me."

She handed the pad back to Elaine and stared at her intently. Her eyes gave Elaine a strange sensation and she caught herself quickly before she blushed. "Are you coming back to pose again?" Elaine now asked casually. "No, not for weeks," Nicole answered, still looking at her with a piercing glance that seemed to recognize something familiar in Elaine.

Elaine sensed the meaning of Nicole's stare—it recalled an almost-forgotten memory of Phyllis. Spontaneously, impelled by a strong need to determine once and for all the extent of her own tendencies, Elaine faced Nicole squarely and said, "Get dressed. We'll have coffee together."

It was cold and businesslike, this matter of having coffee and getting things said out in the open, although strangely exciting in its degree of anticipation. Sorbonne-educated Nicole was not more than twenty but she had thoroughly digested Sartre and Cocteau and had taken the matter of Beat Existentialism quite seriously. She had just returned from a torrid affair with a Parisian café singer and was now anxious to liven up New York's "gay" society with a little French abandon.

"You are an exciting woman," Nicole had remarked intensely, over coffee. "Can you really be a lesbian? But no, you are fooling me."

Elaine had smiled enigmatically. "Why worry about being fooled when it's plain I desire you?"

"Yes, but how? To put on paper?" Nicole was intensely observant. Elaine looked down, not able to say no to her question. "Still, you are difficult to resist," Nicole had added.

Elaine had coldly drained her cup and then gotten up. "Take me home."

Nicole stood, too, their bodies drawn toward each other in

expectation. Then she had put money down on the table to pay the check, quite gallantly, and had escorted Elaine out of the restaurant and down the block to her car.

Nicole drove efficiently, once in a while glancing sidewise at Elaine, who sat quietly beside her, tense in every muscle. She was tense because she found Nicole attractive and this frightened her—it was the first time that Elaine had ever found anyone attractive. Phyllis had not attracted her and, because she had failed to please Phyllis, elaine had experienced an impulse to do something that immediately shocked her and, when she tried to put it to herself in words, even disgusted her; she had not continued even though Phyllis had wrestled with the agony of incompletion and Elaine's own body had trembled to go on.

"What are you saying to yourself?" Nicole asked, turning into the block that led to her apartment.

"Embarrassing things," Elaine said, suddenly looking at her. A sort of blush had formed on her face, but not a shy blush, more like a flush of excitement.

"Tell me upstairs," Nicole smiled.

They barely got upstairs and past the door of Nicole's flat before they lost their forced composure. Elaine was the aggressor, suddenly taking hold of Nicole's shoulder with a demanding hand that turned both of their bodies to meet each other in what was not a kiss but, rather, the sort of strangling embrace into which the slim trunks of two young trees will sometimes entwine—finding themselves so closely rooted that they must become one. Then their mouths drank of each other, not satisfied by the trembling touch of bodies alone, breasts pressed against the softness of other breasts. Elaine realized that this was different from the time with Phyllis—that Nicole lacked both embarrassment and guilt, that she was completely unashamed. This made all the difference. For Nicole, what Elaine desired to do was neither disgusting nor perverted; it was without question the most beautiful physical expression of love that could be shared.

They moved, somehow, to the bed and there continued to embrace, finding avenues through clothing to touch parts of vibrant flesh.

"Lie back," Nicole said impatiently, finding Elaine's strength opposing her efforts to caress her.

"No," Elaine said, refusing to be passive. She brought her mouth to Nicole's throat and forced her to be still, nervously unbuttoning her blouse to feel Nicole's soft bosom, the bosom she had drawn detachedly earlier that afternoon and which now, beneath her hand, felt volatile, like bird's down, warm and quivering and not quite touchable.

Nicole responded with a degree of femininity Elaine had not expected of her hard exterior. It gave Elaine courage to do what she wanted, confident that it would not offend, would not trespass. But she was not lost in the moment—she was apart from it, going through the motions like a scientist performing an experiment. And even in the hour of Nicole's fulfillment, Elaine knew, was positive, that she was not really a lesbian. Nicole admitted it too, reluctantly; Elaine was not changed, not called out of her distant world.

"You do not feel as if you have slept with angels?" Nicole had half-asked, half-stated, wanting to be very sure about Elaine—afraid to begin to love Elaine until she was sure.

Elaine shook her head. "No, I'm not on Cloud Nine. Was I supposed to be? I'm sorry." She sat up, anxious to oblige one more time in the spirit of chivalry that was so innate in her.

Nicole stopped her with a sigh and a wave of her hand. "No, sometimes things are not complete even when they are complete. I think that is the way I would feel toward men . . . "

It wasn't until Peter that Elaine found Nicole's observation quite accurate. Although her times with Peter were utterly incomplete, utterly awkward and even ugly, her love was complete—complete in her desire that he please her, complete in her disappointment when he failed. For brief seconds she was beginning to rise to Cloud Nine.

In the weeks following that first night, Peter made of himself a convenience, even a necessity, and they half moved in together—upstairs and downstairs. He made her follow her diet and made her well enough to go out on picnics and horseback riding with him. For weeks they saw little of John and Mirium, living in a happy world of carefree doodling. It got so he could talk to her for hours and it made her glad to have gotten past the door of his inner world: it was a more downcast world than hers. When he told her about the Army mess it threw her into a rage and it brought her closer to him—Elaine had always cared for underdogs, any underdogs.

And Elaine got over the disappointment of sex, too. She adjusted to it as she adjusted to everything else unpleasant—lumping the pain it caused her with the general pain of her ulcer. It was simple to enjoy Peter, as long as she treated his love-making as a form of self-punishment; her illness had made her frail and everything he did hurt her, but the hurt could be turned into a form of pleasure if she looked at it from the right angle. Once in a while she would stop and ask herself why she was punishing herself and the answer would be—for having been born a woman.

And yet Elaine liked Peter's body, desired it despite constant frustration. He was handsomer than the boys back home, more delicately molded, having the beauty of Greek statues rather than the Anglo-Saxon awkwardness she had disliked so much in men—the large protruding Adam's apple and the bad posture, the hyperpituitary jaw and knotted elbows, the foul smell of just-an-old-shaving-lotion and the bleak look of brown suits that reflected a genetic tendency toward color-blindness. Peter was immaculately clean and conservatively dressed, and always with color and a distinct taste for what was refined and pleasing to the eye. Elaine had been proud to take him home to Dad.

They got married at City Hall and invited only John and Mirium as witnesses, thinking to tell their parents afterwards, because they wanted this moment to be all theirs, did not want to share it with relatives, mothers and fathers, all weeping and excited about their young ones pairing off. They had a quiet ceremony and then went home again and John called out the neighborhood.

"Hey, Peter's married Elaine," John shouted down the street, and windows opened. The Bowery- bohemians stuck their heads out, bearded and unbearded heads of men, of women, thin and drawn and with long, dirty-yellow hair or stringy black hair—and the heads of neat young men in advertising and the beautiful heads of models and actresses, and the heads of ethnics—of Italians and Puerto Ricans and Polacks and Jews. The windows rumbled on both sides of the block and the tenement dwellers looked out curiously, hearing John's loud boom over the rock-'n-roll on their radios and the barking of puppies. "Hey, Elaine's married Peter!" John stopped on the steps of their house and shouted again. "There's a party. Bring your own bottle!" His message was relayed by three or four echoing voices in both directions of the block.

The neighborhood delinquents took him up on the offer first and were received by Mirium like upstanding citizens, so they refrained from wrecking the house. John turned up the stereo into a public address system and Mirium passed out boxes of confetti and streamers' to members of The Dragons—as the boys called themselves on the back of their leather jackets—and the juveniles ran out into the street with them, dressing up the stoops and the parked cars, hurling wild *vacchero* whoops in their best Latin manner. The party grew through the afternoon and the bongo-drum crowd arrived. Peter and Elaine were the only ones missing, hiding from the crowd in Elaine's basement. Then Elaine finally got around to wiring the news home and Peter telephoned his parents.

They hugged each other tightly as Peter dialed, the spirit of John's party touching them even though they were alone. "Hey, Mom, I got married!" Peter said when she answered, caught up in the excitement of the moment. He was like a boy again—but only for an instant—for quickly he realized that he had broken the news too suddenly. It was too late. The ritual of quieting his anxious parents followed.

"They're in hysterics," he said finally. He cradled the receiver distractedly and sat and tried to puzzle it out.

Elaine had expected it. Parents always took sudden news badly. She expected her own parents to be hurt but for her it didn't matter—she had never been close to them. Moreover, she wasn't marrying a devout member of the congregation whom she had dated for ten years. Nothing short of that would have kept her dad from being unpleasantly surprised. He would accept Peter to the family, of course, would even welcome him, although Peter might be a Methodist or a

Jehovah's Witness or even a Jew.   However, Elaine could not even hope to please him in that way because Peter wasn't at all religious. That she had married someone who didn't believe in Christ would wound him deeply, and someone who didn't even believe in God—that would absolutely crush him.   Elaine knew her dad would say nothing about it and yet she had given up hoping for his acceptance.

But Peter hadn't given up on his parents.   He hadn't seen them all year but now he wanted badly that they approve of Elaine.

"When do I meet them?" Elaine sighed patiently.

"Tomorrow," he said. "We're invited to dinner."

She went over and pressed his head to her thigh, rubbing the lines away from his forehead. "Don't worry, I'll make them like me."

The next morning they took the train to the suburbs, in the heat of summer, feeling sticky with sweat and grime. The noise of the subway kept them from talking and the ride seemed to take forever. It gave Elaine a headache. When they came out into the fresh air again, she could barely walk the six blocks to the house.   Then they saw the Claussons waiting, sitting on chairs in their small front yard and when Peter waved they came down to meet them on the sidewalk.

"This is Elaine," Peter said proudly and both of them embraced her. They were cold, determined embraces, from two people desperately determined to accept her.

Peter Sr. said, "Well, she's beautiful, Peter."

"welcome to the family," Peter's mother said dramatically.

They went inside, forced in their light tone, and gave Elaine a grand tour of the house, displaying all the various innovations since Peter had last been there: a new gadget, a costly partition, the expensive flower pattern of the bedroom wallpaper.

"You keep an immaculate house," Elaine said to Peter's mother, trying to sound wifey and feminine. Inwardly, she rebelled in all her being against the homemaker stereotype that Peter's mother expected Peter's wife to be. The short, round woman smiled nervously but with a trace of pride.

"Let's go on to the garage," Peter Sr. said, also encouraged by Elaine's comment.

"May I sit down a moment?" Elaine said weakly, bringing one hand to her forehead. "I'm afraid I've gotten a headache." She found the couch nearby with her hand and eased herself into it. Peter went to her side. "Are you sure you're all right?"

"Just a dizzy spell," Elaine said, trying to recover. The strain of the visit was becoming too much for her nervous disposition.

"Elaine's been ill," Peter explained to his parents. They stood looking at her, a concern for Elaine in their eyes but beneath it, an agitated expression of concern for their son.

"May I get you an aspirin?" Peter's mother volunteered.

"No, thank you," Elaine said, rubbing her brow. "But, could I have a glass of milk?"

"Why, yes," his mother said, a little puzzled, and went toward the kitchen.

"Cream, mother, if you have any," Peter shouted after her. "Elaine has an ulcer." Then he reached in his pocket for the antacid pills he always carried for her.

His father sat down in the easy chair opposite the couch and regarded them. Peter Sr. was a tall, dark man with a Scandinavian square head and jaw around which the flesh clung in well-marked grooves. He had almost no gray hair and yet was over fifty—an easygoing, comfortable-looking man in a large suit with large pockets. He sat and waited, observing them, especially Elaine, as he began to stuff his pipe.

Peter fretted as Peter always fretted over Elaine's fainting spells. He took her hand and sat patting it, ready to jump the minute Elaine should utter a request of any kind.

His mother arrived with a glass of pure cream which Elaine took and drank slowly.

"Perhaps you'll feel better at dinner," Mother Clausson said.

When Elaine had recovered sufficiently, they went into the dining room.

Elaine could not eat dinner. Mother Clausson had fixed a beautiful spiced ham, something way off Elaine's rigid diet. She could not touch the salad, nor the firmly cooked vegetables, nor the specially baked nut bread. She took a potato and a lump of butter and ate slowly.

"I hope you're not on Elaine's diet too," his mother said cautiously, looking suspiciously at Elaine.

"No, Mother," Peter said. "Elaine's a great cook."

"Have you been ill a long time?" Peter Sr. broke in.

"I don't know," Elaine answered without looking up. "It's a silent ulcer—hard to diagnose and cure."

When they left to go home that night Elaine was almost a total wreck. She was ill for the next week. Meanwhile, Peter's mother called often, concerned and impatient to see her son's living conditions and to be invited to dinner. Peter put his parents off saying that they planned to move to the suburbs as soon as they could. He shrugged off his father's offer of money, not wanting to be dependent, and consoled himself over the loss of his parents' approval by seeking out Elaine. But Elaine took her failure badly, as she took all failure. She was not the wife Peter deserved—she wasn't even strong enough to clean her own apartment.

Meeting Elaine's parents was a longer ordeal. A long-distance phone call came from Massachusetts as a result of Elaine's wire and they were invited up for a weekend. They accepted when Elaine was well enough to go.

Peter had never quite realized that he had been born a freethinker—New Yorkers being, for the most part, not too religious. It came to him as a shock when he went to New England with Elaine. Her family lived in a small town across from Roger Williams' Rhode Island and were themselves the victims of harmless bias, as Northern Baptists encircled by a hotbed of Lutherans. This made them twice as determined to be Baptists. "They'll resent anyone who's not in their congregation," Elaine had explained laughingly to Peter on the bus. "It's a game all the Protestants play against each other. Then they get upset because the Catholics are taking over New England."

Elaine's careless talk made the trip less tedious for him but it wore her out. She was really quite tense about bringing him home to Dad. Then the highway became familiar to her and, from the bus, she saw the green fields she had loved so dearly and had missed all year, then the blue-green bay and the white wooden houses of Main Street. For a moment she was jubilant about being physically home—not because being close to her family but because treading on native soil.

Elaine's brother picked up at the depot. The family had bought a new car since she had been there last; his freckled, red-topped frame barely fit in it and his curly head was an inch from the ceiling. "Hello, Sis," he said, then shook hands with Peter and started the car again.

All of Elaine's immediate relatives—there were about twenty of them, including the brothers and sisters-in-law and assorted children—had gathered for a reunion and were waiting to have dinner as soon as they arrived. Peter was hurriedly introduced to all of them and finally to Elaine's father—her mother being busy in the kitchen with the other women and unable to come out—and he shook Peter's hand with the best show of warm friendship he could muster. Elaine's father was not a demonstrative man, a farmer by tradition and, for a short time, until Elaine's mother had developed tuberculosis, an agricultural missionary to India.

He shook Peter's hand, looking not quite at him but over him, to some great beyond that perhaps betrayed a touch of near-sightedness for which he would not wear corrective lenses. The family resemblance was clear between him and Elaine's brothers—the only difference being in his hair which was a blond-white—but only his eyes resembled Elaine's. She was too delicate to be his true offspring; he had much of a skeleton about him although he was not overly thin; and all of his bones were knobbed.

Peter tried to greet him over the noise of the grandchildren, but it didn't matter. His comments were not missed.

They went into the large dining room and the adults sat at a long colonial table while the children were accommodated at various tables around the room. Peter, as the latest addition, sat at the right of Elaine's father. Everyone became quiet at once and *Grace* was said and then the noise spontaneously resumed and continued all weekend. In many ways, it was as if Peter's addition to the family had made no real impression—as if Peter did not really exist. . . .

6.

Had Peter existed? Elaine heard his footsteps on the ceiling and decided that he had. If he hadn't sent all her clothes to the laundromat, now she and Nicole would have gone upstairs to keep him company. But she was too weak, anyway. She had finally made sense out of the disorder he had caused among her paints and now Nicole was waiting in her chair again, ready to pose. But today neither the painting nor the model seemed the same. Elaine paused and tried to see what was wrong: the sunbeams were not bouncing off Nicole in a way that she could capture them. Peter's footsteps on the ceiling were interrupting her entire existence.

"What is wrong?" Nicole asked, seeing Elaine put down her palette knife again with no intention of using it. "Are you not well?"

"No, I'm sick," Elaine told her, then tried to smile. But she could not look at Nicole honestly. She closed her eyes and stumbled back to bed, lying down again.

"Is there something I can do?" Nicole went to sit by her side with concern.

"No, nothing," Elaine sighed and patted her hand fondly. Nicole took Elaine's hand impulsively and kissed the palm. "Don't." Elaine said and withdrew her hand, but not roughly. She patted Nicole's cheek. *"Pardonez moi, ma cherie."*

Nicole sighed and shrugged, *"Il n'importe pas."* Then, standing, she said, *"C'est lui, n'est ce pas?"* She looked to the ceiling, to Peter's footsteps.

Elaine nodded. "I wondered if he would come back."

Nicole shrugged again and extended her hand. "I think I will leave you alone for a while. *Alors, au demain?"*

"If you wish," Elaine said, too weak to take Nicole's hand one more time.

Nicole hesitated for a moment, waiting for Elaine to change her mind but when she did not, she took her sweater and purse and left.

It was nice to have silence, except for Peter's footsteps. Elaine lay with her eyes open, listening to him as he crossed the floor back and forth upstairs, busy with his resurrection of a crucified past. She hoped he wasn't bringing back to life a bloody mess.

Beginning again: the thought haunted her, too. Peter had come to save her from the monster of unmarked time, time that knew neither night nor day except in terms of exhausted sleep and intense work—and hunger—always hunger vulturing in her bowels. The painting wasn't much to show for all her sacrifice; in fact, it was hardly anything at all to show. It was sick, myopic—strabismused and color-blind.

She let her eyes close, eyes that ached around and behind the eyeballs and saw nothing but her own red blood, red capillaries between her mind and the shining bars of sunlight—yellow sunlight from the basement window. Peter had come back. She ached to welcome him, ached to cry for joy—but she had no strength for tears, no moisture left in her eyes, and her welcoming would be hard because she was afraid to be glad, afraid to be tender.

She was about to doze off when she heard John's heavy knock on the door. "Come in but I'm half naked," she warned, then watched him force his way through the rubble.

"Just thought I'd look in on you," John said. "Is Pete around?"

"Upstairs, working himself to death," she pointed. "Sit awhile."

John found a chair in the middle of the floor and took the load off his feet. "Glad he's back?"

She shrugged, sitting up. "Say, do me a favor, will you? Turn that monstrosity to the wall." She pointed to the painting.

"About time," he said with an air of relief and got up immediately to follow her instructions.

"Had a good lecture?" she asked.

"Fair. Couldn't seem to make myself clear on some points, though." He sat down again. "I got to worrying about you kids."

"John—" Elaine started to make a long speech and then stopped— "just mind your own business."

"When I'm through minding yours," he came back at her, then got up again and stretched. His hands thumped the low ceiling. "Shall I send Pete down? Isn't it about time for your formula?"

"I wail every three hours," she said. "But you can tell him he's welcome to my shower when he's through."

"Good enough," John beamed and went toward the door. "Incidentally, Mirium want you both up for pea soup tonight."

"Ask my stomach again when it wakes up," she sighed, then, with more feeling, "Thanks."

She watched him struggle with the half-broken door, then lay down again to dream—but not or long, since John relayed her message to Peter with a whoop as he came up the stairs. "Hey! She said you could use her shower!"

Peter returned the whoop and dropped everything, plunging down the stairs. He burst through her door with an excited expectation only to find her facing the wall, with her back to him. "So soon?" she commented blandly.

"It's dirty work upstairs," Peter said awkwardly. "Thought I'd go back to it later." He waited another moment for her to say something, then went to finda towel in his suitcase, and his electric razor. He stopped again by the bathroom door. "Aren't you going to take one, too?"

"Whatever for?" she shrugged, her back still to him.

"Cleanliness is next to Godliness," he mottoed and closed the door behind him.

He came out a half-hour later in his shorts, not bothering to put on the rest of his clothes just yet, all shaved and bathed and cologned, the towel around his neck, bare-chested and trying to appear as *Hollywoodish* as possible with his San Francisco roof tan. But she was still not looking. He decided to be bold and sat on her bed, taking a deep noisy breath to indicate that he was there.

It made no impression on her. As a last resort he bent over and kissed her behind the ear. She pulled away and dug her face in the pillow. This made Peter impatient and for a minute he thought of pulling the covers off her but then decided to curb his baser instincts. He would wait and convince her. "Elaine—" he said, testing.

"Please go away, Peter," she said into the pillow.

"I want to talk to you," he whispered, not moving.

"There's nothing to say," she answered. It was not a cold statement, not an angry sentence. There was weariness in her voice. "Why didn't you write?" she asked after a long wait.

"I was being mean," he stated.

"Well, it's too late to mourn spilt turpentine," she sighted, turning to face him. Her face was red where the traces of tears had streaked her cheeks. She looked at him silently, calmly, without anger. "You're six weeks too late, Peter."

"You mean, about Nicole?" He looked at her. She nodded and he looked down. "I know. I'm sorry."

He wanted her, needed to take all of her, craved her so much he couldn't think clearly, distracted by the sight of her white skin, her bare whiteness where his borrowed shirt exposed her collarbone, white skin slightly freckled with a peach coloring that made her more delicious to his ravenous eyes. He convinced himself fully that she felt the same way about him, that Elaine couldn't talk sensibly now because she craved him to take her. This sound argument for yielding to impulse filled him with righteous action and he covered her body with his weight, not waiting to kiss or caress her.

It worked in a way, although she was fighting herself to keep from responding. He felt her body tremble under him and he held her more firmly, biting the back of her neck where it joined her shoulder.

"Peter, for God's sake," she pleaded.

"We can't talk first, Elaine" he answered in her ear.

For a moment she seemed to yield to the logic of it then she froze, turning her dace away and making her body fall still on the bed, dead, not fighting him at all—a cold, rigid sort of pose that made him realize he could take her but it would be rape.

He stopped, fighting with himself, and then he knew he couldn't wait for her to want him even if she would hate him for it. He sat up long enough to remove the blanket that barred his way and then took her again, kissing her unresponsive lips and her cool, soft breasts with a savage urgency, relieving himself in the cool warmth of her, hating himself and hating her for spoiling this beautiful moment.

She slid her face away and kept staring at the wall, distant from the whole act, with the sort of will power that only Elaine could be capable of. He knew she ached to respond, knew by the tenseness in her body that she was fighting the welcome acceptance of his firm presence inside her.

"John should have lent you more money," she said when he was through, coldly, blankly. "It would have been more decent to go buy a whore."

"That wouldn't have been the same," he answered with a measure of arrogance but still with sincerity.

It would not have been the same. He hadn't flown three thousand miles to take just any woman. No one but Elaine would do. He stood and began to put on the clothes he had brought with him from the bathroom, feeling refreshed and strong and self-satisfied, able to think and to talk again. He had the upper hand now. Elaine still lay quietly on the bed, not looking at him. With a merciful festure he covered her so she would not catch cold.

"Do you think you can disappear for a year and then come back and take up right where you left off?" Tears were selling up in her eyes again, nervous tears—not those of grief and broken hearts because Elaine's heart had been shattered long long ago, the first time some nurse had dropped her from her cradle.

"Why not?" he shrugged lightly, buckling his belt. "You still love me." But he wan't being light about it.

She slapped him—not yard, just enough to show how seriously she felt about the word love—and then she watched him, waiting for him to make the next move. But he didn't. He couldn't. Suddenly he needed to talk to her—he hadn't talked to her all year.

"Elaine, I love you," he said intensely. "As I never loved you before." He stopped. The sentence was corny. But there were two years behind it, two very serious years.

"Why did you go, Peter?" Elaine finally broke down, turning away from him again to face the wall with a look that was sadder than crying.

"I lost my nerve," he said. There was no guilt in his voice, only a factual tone, a cold approach to the truth. "I began to think you weren't good enough for me—that our whole life wasn't good enough for me." This was not an arrogant statement and he knew she understood it wasn't. "Mom's phone calls, and the prospect of supporting your ulcer for the rest of my life. I suddenly decided I was just punishing myself, trying to get back at myself for the whole Army mess by marrying you."

He stopped, waiting for her to react in some way, but she merely listened. "Do you know what I mean?" he continued. "It really had nothing to do with you. It was being twenty-nine and going on thirty with no kind of security, no future ahead of me and a wife I couldn't ever hope to please, a stranger I sometimes got to make love to, who let herself be taken with the best possible show of self-sacrifice she could muster up for the occasion. Do I make myself clear?"

"Very clear," she said. There was silence. He knew that he had suddenly revived the past—had brought back the awful months wherein they had both retired from the world and from each other—Elaine, in her painting and in her ulcer that required lots of sleep and little sex—Peter, in his involved project of constructing a bigger and better stereo system while living on unemployment. Even John and Mirium had stopped being asked to come around. Their life had converged into two separate camps: Peter's, on the floor near the kitchen surrounded by bolts and screws and wire and burlap; Elaine's, at the easel by the window, blocked by cans of paint and turpentine.

They had been waiting out a cold war against the reality of living in a mixed-up society neither of them could accept, planning nothing because 'The Bomb' might suddenly be dropped. One day he had slammed the door behind him as he left to walk off steam—and then he just kept on walking, all the way to the bus depot.

He had deserted Elaine, and he knew that she knew it. He had sent her money every month to ease his conscience—from Philadelphia, from Miami, from Dallas, and finally from San Francisco. But he couldn't write to her. He had nothing to say. He was just waiting on tables.

The past flashed before both of them and now Elaine put her hand on her eyes, closing them for a moment and feeling the strain on her forehead. "You'll have to give me time, Peter," she said. "It's not easy to give up Nicole for you—not easy at all."

"I know," he grunted with a trace of bitterness. "She pleases you and I don't. But Elaine, if you'd only let me—"

"It's not the same," she interrupted him. "There's all the difference in the world."

He shrugged. "Well, I'll be sleeping upstairs, in case you decide to join me."

"I'll think about it," she said distantly, then waited for him to leave.

Peter left the basement but the room, and Elaine, was still full of him. She twisted to one side, giving in to the cramp she had been holding back while he was there. She had not wanted to give in to him, had not wanted to let herself be pleased. It was too soon. He had not proved that he deserved her. And Nicole had deserved her; she had proven it easily.

Peter had been wrong about Nicole. Nicole had never fulfilled Elaine, despite the long hours she had spent trying to fulfill her, despite Elaine's wish to be fulfilled by her because Elaine felt Nicole deserved her. Neither man nor woman had yet fulfilled Elaine . . .

Nicole had come around to visit six weeks ago, expecting to be a friend to both Elaine and Peter, now that they were married. She had just returned from a long vacation in Paris and knew nothing about Peter's having left Elaine. She had not expected to find Elaine alone and her first reaction had been to want to leave so that she might not be tempted to relight an old torch. She had wanted no part of the role of mistress. But she had found Elaine painting, and half starved. Peter's checks had been on the table, uncashed. Elaine had neither the time for the strength to go to the grocery store. The kitchen was too filthy to cook in, the bed had dirty sheets.

"*Merde!*" Nicole had exclaimed, "are you living somewhere else?" She had arrived dressed to the hilt, as usual, in the latest Parisian schoolgirl fashion—in green and black wool, with wool knee-length socks and funny leather shoes. It made her look dashingly feminine, with that special severe charm that *Jeanne D'Arc* might have had when she got all those men to follow her into battle.

"Wade on in," Elaine had said, not turning from her painting. "No,

I don't live elsewhere." She was standing in the clear space, wearing a wrinkled shirt and a pair of jeans that smelled as if they had clothed all of George Washington's army.

Nicole found a path for her feet and went to sit on the chair. "Where's Peter?"

"Peter's left me," Elaine answered. Her voice was slightly bitter.

"For good?" Nicole exclaimed with a spontaneous tone of regret in the way that she might take the unhappy news of someone's death, someone she barely knew.

"He didn't say," Elaine shrugged. She stepped back to appraise her work better—it was a non-objective mess with too much color and no form, unarranged and full of anger. "Step over here and pose awhile, will you?" Elaine sighed, turning to Nicole. "This badly needs a model."

"No, I cannot stay," Nicole answered with a degree of impatience. She could not stand filth and the stench of the place was overpowering her. "How can you live like such a pig?"

"It's easy," Elaine smiled, wiping her brush on a paint-stained portion of a pair of old panties she now used as a rag. "Just let it all grow around you and don't bother lifting a finger to change it."

"Come to my place and take a shower," Nicole said, standing again, anxious to leave the basement.

"What? And leave my masterpiece? All right, you talked me into it," Elaine said, putting down the rag.

They waded out of the basement again and Elaine took a deep breath of sun-filled smog, noticing that it was midday. "Do you know, I haven't been out all week," she said.

Nicole led the way to her station wagon and Elaine got in and sank deep in the seat, suddenly realizing how dirty her clothes were and trying to hide herself from the sight of oncoming pedestrians.

"You can borrow a dress at my house," Nicole said, getting into the driver's seat. She started the car and pulled out quickly, anxious to get Elaine to a shower. She could not stand seeing someone she had once found attractive enough to sleep with looking so awfully derelict. It was an insult to her good taste.

"Why did Peter go away?" she asked as they rode. It was simply in the cause of human interest. Nicole had no designs on Elaine, not after seeing how she lived now.

"Because I'm frigid, I guess." Elaine shrugged. "How should I know? He hasn't written." She rested her head on the back of the seat and closed her eyes. "I don't want to talk about it."

Nicole made the trip across to her Bleecker Street apartment very quickly, found a legal parking place and stopped. Elaine piled wearily out of the car and followed her upstairs, taking the three flights with great effort. Then they entered Nicole's meticulously neat flat. for a few brief weeks, it had once been Elaine's home, too, before he had rented the basement. Now, she wasted no time in finding the shower.

When Elaine came out, wrapped in a large whie bath towel. Nicole had put out an entirely new set of clothes for her. She was making a cold lunch in the kitchen for them. Elaine did not bother changing but walked, barefooted, to sit at the kitchen table. The hot water and no sleep had made her groggy and her stomach was burning again. Nicole put a plate of tuna fish and canned asparagus in front of her and then sat down on her side and began to eat, not saying anything.

Elaine nibbled at her food and watched Nicole, discerning a blush that had formed beneath her dark Riviera tan. Being alone with Elaine was a strain on Nicole's emotions. It recalled for a moment those very intense two months they had once spent together here.

"How have you been?" Elaine asked cautiously.

Nicole shrugged and sank her fork into a chunk of tuna. She stopped eating for a moment and looked up. "And you? What are you going to do with yourself?"

"I guess I'll wait for Peter to come back," Elaine sighed.

"Then you still love him?" Nicole prompted warily.

"I don't know," Elaine answered. The whole subject of Peter was unpleasant for Elaine. She did not want to think of Peter, had successfully avoided asking herself all year just why their marriage had flopped so badly. She had spent her time painting on a canvas, the same canvas, over and over again, destroying each theme and replacing it with a different one—with new colors and new designs. It was like

Penelope's tapestry, woven to stall of the suitors while she waited for Odysseus to come home. No Elaine wondered if it would take Peter twenty years.

"Well," Nicole said, finishing her lunch and shoving the plate away, "at least, my pride has been saved. I was not the only one to fail you."

"No, Peter couldn't please me either," Elaine smiled distantly.

Nicole stood up and went to the stove, slightly flustered. "I'll pour you some coffee then I will take you home."

Elaine accepted the cup, poured lots of milk in it and drank it slowly, looking up at Nicole a few times over the rim. Nicole's eyes were looking down in front of her, fixed on the table.

"It's awkward, my being here, isn't it?" Elaine said finally, putting her cup down.

"Yes," Nicole nodded, not looking up. Her fingers were sliding nervously around her saucer, back and forth.

Elaine stood, but lingered. "Well, I guess I'd better get dressed."

She analyzed her own reluctance to leave: Peter had been away a long time and might never decide to come back; and Nicole was still unfinished business, an episode without a proper ending. Peter had come to interrupt it and had taken Elaine away from Nicole. True, Elaine had moved away from Nicole's to her own apartment, but it was only because she had wanted to be free to think more about it—this idea that she might be a lesbian.

She had married Peter because she had finally decided that she wasn't—but now a doubt was coming to her again, seeing Nicole, suddenly wanting Nicole. It prompted her to do something she had never done before—be aggressive. She walked deliberately to Nicole's side of the table and bent down, lightly kissing her lips.

Nicole stood up, blushing. "Come on, now, get dressed."

"Not unless you insist," Elaine said. She was not behaving like her indifferent self at all—a year alone had changed her, and the year before that with Peter. She was identifying with Peter now, playing the role of the male more than ever. She moved closer, maneuvering to kiss Nicole once more.

Nicole kept her at arm's length. "I do insist," she said. "I don't like

Elaine to be "butch."

Nothing more was said about it in the weeks following. Elaine spoke little anyway: she had grown slovenly about carrying on meaningful conversations, had grown far too introverted in the past three years. Still, she fought the growing blankness in her mind, the slower-motion thought that kept her silent and almost always half-asleep—or was it higher-speed thought, so fast that her mind could not grasp and remember things as they sped by.

The only moments that were truly real were those when she painted, or made love to Nicole—and those moments too were quickly becoming blurred. She could not quite explain what was causing this, this seeing the entire world in front of her ten feet further away from her than it really was, so that she had to pinpoint objects with her eyes as if she were looking at a distant horizon. Perhaps her thought-patterns were acquiring bad habits from disuse mostly, and from starvation. More and more often she seemed just to want to sit and not cope with any of it, just lie in bed and be ill with some disease or other called hypochondria. But she forced herself to get up by telling herself that she must paint, must accomplish, but even this 3was not as strong an urge any more.

Conversely, Nicole thrived on Elaine's presence. "Ah, you are wonderful!" she would exclaim, taking both of Elaine's ears and shaking her head fondly. "You make my whole world sharp and clear. I want to write a poem."

She wrote several, in two languages, and then registered for evening college to continue her education. She also helped Elaine tackle the job of cleaning the basement. They did the best they could and Elaine moved back in so she could work more intensely. Nicole came every other day to pose and to see that Elaine had enough to eat. They were still wary of each other and little by little it was dawning on both of them that Elaine was not in love.

"I don't want you unless you are really a lesbian," Nicole said very often, almost hoping to evoke some sort of assurance from Elaine. But Elaine never answered her statement.

Was she a lesbian?

Elaine suddenly knew that she was not as she now lay fighting the lingering presence of Peter. He had nearly fulfilled her and she had been seconds from it although she had not wanted to be. The realization that she had finally responded to him in spite of herself panicked her, broke the slow-motion train of thought, slowed the speeding in her mind, made the slow track fast and the fast track slow, focused the world in a reversal that jolted her back to the present, back to life. She was suddenly strong, suddenly herself.

7.

Peter sauntered upstairs to John's apartment, feeling full of the world and with a need to burst into long monologues, to tell John and Mirium all his plans now that he was back. It was great to be back.

"Barge in," John invited, "you're expected." They were having lunch—pea soup as usual.

"Thanks." Peter pulled up a chair at the table and Mirium poured him a serving. It was more like green lentil chicken stew, savory and quite filling, but needed cooling. Peter took time to look around him. The baby was sleeping on the bed and the place was a little more tidy than that morning, no longer in a depressed state of confusion. It was obvious they were planing to move, but just *when* was the question.

"How did you make out with Elaine?" Mirium asked.

Peter shrugged. "She'll come around."

"I invited her up to eat," John said, bread in his mouth.

"I don't think she feels well," Peter said. He felt a little guilty. He had probably made her ill. Her physique was too delicate for much of that sort of treatment. He determined to be more considerate in the future.

John grunted and let a pause fall. "Mimi and I have been working on a plan of attack."

"I wish you'd keep out of it," Peter said mildly. He wanted to be tactful about not requiring their help.

"nonsense, Pete," John said. "It's plain you need help. Elaine's a strange case. Look—we figured out a way to run interference on Nicole." He put down his spoon emphatically.

"But I really don't need any help," Peter said. He still didn't want to turn them down too harshly. He was grateful that they cared so much about him—like family.

"We're not taking no for an answer," John dismissed his reply with a wave of his hand. Then, more emphatically, he bent over. "We don't have much time, boy, I got word they're starting to tear down the end of the block this week. This house hasn't got much longer for this world."

Mirium nodded to his words.

"You mean—next week, we all have to move?" Peter looked at them in alarm. He hadn't expected the wreckers so soon.

"Can't tell," John sighed, wiping sweat from his forehead. "Anyway, if you don't get Elaine back this week things are going to be much too complicated later—when she has to move to heaven knows where, maybe even back to Nic's place."

"We mustn't let that happen, Pete," Mirium echoed. "Please let us help you."

"All right," Peter yielded. "What do you suggest?"

John broke off another piece of Italian bread and stuffed his mouth, then talked seriously as he chewed, looking much like a general. "I met this young beatnik on my way back home," he said. "I told him he could come and sleep here—a young kid from Indianapolis, ran away from home two months ago and has been selling instant poetry in the Village art show—thinks he's a writer. A real gone character, half starved and anxious to please anyone who's nice to him."

He paused, to let the description sink in. "Now, I figure there's only one way to get Elaine back and that's to disillusion her about women. Now, this kid, Donald's his name, is willing to run interference. He's going to play queer and get Nicole off guard. While they're off being playmates you ought to have plenty of time to work on Elaine—once she decides that Nic and Don are pairing off, well, that'll be the end of their hot romance." He stopped, satisfied, and took a drink of ice water.

"You should be writing for the pulps," Peter commented dryly.

"No, thanks, John, I'm sure Nicole won't fall for it, and I wouldn't buy it, either. I'll be better off getting Elaine my way."

"But it won't do any harm to try," Mirium said. "Don's coming over any minute. He hasn't any other place to sleep."

"Listen to me, Pete. You don't understand lesies like I do," John argued his position. "They flirt and camp like mad just to prove they're still women. Don'll bulldoze her to bed before she knows it."

"Think of what a favor we'll be doing Nicole," Mirium interjected. "Do you want that poor girl to go on being a lesbian all her life?"

"That's right," John said. "Don might be her golden opportunity."

"Count me out of it," Peter said. "That's one way I don't want to fight."

But it was too late. The beatnik now made his appearance. Even as Peter spoke, Don stood at the door and boomed in a happy, happy voice, "Greetings and salutations, friends, Romans, countrymen."

"Pray enter," John waved, himself lost in the tone of the modern medieval ceremony.

Donald entered stiffly. He was a very young man, about twenty, nearly all in rags, unshaven and unbathed, but with good posture and an excellent physique—a carrot-topped all-American football player gone wrong.

Peter turned to look at him and then shrank back in his seat and shuddered, mentally cursing John for his tendency to always overcomplicate life, making it into a blueprint for some large atomic stockpile. "Do you really expect Nicole will believe that character is queer?" He addressed his comment to Mirium who was still seated at the table.

John caught the remark. "Wait till he's bathed, shaved and perfumed," he said. "What do you expect? He's been sleeping in doorways."

"I am prepared to serve my country," Donald saluted. The bags under his eyes betrayed a lack of sleep that may have accounted for his drunken stupor. He did not smell of alcohol. His stiff posture was broken only by an occasional violent attack of scratching.

"The bathtub's over there." John pointed to the kitchen. "Throw your clothes in the fireplace. Mirium'll give you new ones." With that, he went back to finish his meal and everyone shifted their chairs so that Donald could remove his clothes in private.

Peter began to laugh, loudly and without interruption. John's plan was a scream—a big, manufactured monstrosity to find a use for someone who needed a place to sleep. Always trying to kill two birds with one stone, John, in this case, was helping Donald get back on his feet and helping Peter at the same time. It was very funny. But the funniest of it was that the plan might work after all.

Nicole was too intelligent to fall for it, but she might use Donald to give up Elaine—something John didn't quite understand about lesbians and Peter did: they were chivalrous like the old fairy princes. Nicole had given up Elaine once before and Peter was certain she was staying now only because Elaine refused to give her up. No matter how John planned it or how Peter looked at it, it was Elaine who had to decide whether to be a lesbian or a wife. He continued to laugh, euphorically, not really finding it a joke.

"I do not appreciate the humor," Donald said, seated in the bathtub.

"I'm sorry," Peter said, gasping for breath.

"I'll bring you some jeans," Mirium said, getting up and going to the cedar chest in the small room they used as a large closet. She and John always kept a variety of sizes in old clothing there, for just such occurrences as this. They were known around the neighborhood as the Beatnik Salvation Army. She brought them over to the bathtub, turning her eyes away. Donald emerged a clean man. Next, John let him borrow his razor.

"What do you know about Jean Cocteau," Peter asked as Donald transformed himself into a wholesome human being again.

"Everything," Donald answered. "I *am* Orpheus. I'm also versed in Gertrude Stein."

"Good," Peter approved, "at least you'll appeal to her intellect."

"Let's hope she appeals to mine," Donald answered.

"Say, were you this way back home?" Peter asked facetiously.

"Of course not," Donald replied in like manner, getting the last of his two-week beard off. "One doesn't dare affectation in the wilds of Indianapolis."

Peter decided Don fit the description "snippy intellectual," the insecure, half "gay" young man who waits shiftlessly for the draft and makes his environment into a great debris—date-raping the local virgins, raking at the arty bars, beating up the queers who might mistake him for one of them, growing a beard and staying bathless to prove his masculinity, adopting all the worst ideas of dog-eat-dog in a temporary though futile attempt to be as vicious as the next guy—because the good he saw in himself seemed impractical, seemed too painful to develop to its fullest.

Don finished shaving now and dabbed his chin with a towel, admiring his clean, wholesome face in the mirror. "Now do you think I'm pretty enough, dearie?" he swished at Peter.

"Disgustingly so, sweet," Peter grimaced with a large measure of hostility. He disliked all the nastiness Don stood for—his big super-male haughtiness and holier-than-thou attitudes that were the outcome, not of his intelligence or intellect, but of his middle-class roots now running wild in Bohemia.

"Say, what's your wife's girl friend like? Is she a derrick?" Don asked haughtily.

"No, she's very feminine," Peter answered, suddenly finding himself defending Nicole.

"Oh, then your wife's the derrick?" Don said, then laughed at his own question.

"Elaine's no derrick, either," Peter said firmly. He found himself getting quite hot under the collar—one more remark and he was ready to . . . well, he didn't know quite what he would be ready to do. It wasn't worth fighting over. It was just his own rotten mood, not Don at all.

"Come on over here and we'll form the plan of attack," John said, his notebook out to write down the schedule. "Now, the four of us will fix up the second floor tonight—get all the furniture back down, make it livable, just like it was last year. That's the first step."

"For this I needed a bath?" Don complained.

"Have you eaten?" Mirium asked him.

"No," Don said reproachfully. She disappeared again and came back with a bowl of pea soup which he began to eat standing up, as he listened to John. "The plan sounds asenine but continue," he interjected. Peter echoed him silently.

"Never mind what it sounds like," John said with annoyance. "The important thing's whether it will work."

"Well, Johnny-o, as long as you supply the pad and the padding I'll go along," Donald said. He had given up trying to spoon the pea soup and now put the bowl to his mouth and drank the rest of it. "But this Nic had better not be a dog. I dig no dogs."

"My wife has excellent taste," Peter insisted.

Donald gave him a skeptical look up and down. "That I don't believe."

Peter forced himself to ignore the remark. "I suppose two weeks at the local charities are what's making you vicious," he commented, trying to be big about his ability to stand insults but at the same time showing his own feline claws.

"Screw you," Don said, not being able to take a good repartee with as much composure.

"Cut it out, both of you," John interrupted. "Let's get started. We've stored some of your furniture in our spare room, Pete. The rest's piled up on the wall in the basement. But first, we've got to clean the place, from top to bottom."

Peter reluctantly began to roll of his sleeves, looking sidewise at Don, afraid to turn his back on him. They both recognized a state of armed truce.

"Give me your ticket and I'll go pick up the laundry," Mirium said to Peter. He did so and then looked to John for the next step.

"We have a household helper," John assured them. "I built me a special Bowery vacuum cleaner. We'll get rid of the filth down there in no time flat."

"It'll still take scrubbing," Peter said. He was pessimistic this afternoon. He decided it was because there was too much interference going on. He would rather have solved all his problems himself, but

John was outnumbering him, as always.

They rigged up John's new contraption, built out of scraps from three old vacuums and a large fire hose that reached all the way downstairs and around the rooms without moving the motor from its stationary place in John's workroom. It picked up all the spare dirt and light woodwork and left the place clean enough to scrub except for the middle of the floor where Peter had already collected the large garbage when he had cleaned that morning. That, they carried down to the cans outside.

Mirium returned with the bag of laundry, put it aside and rushed to fill the tub in the kitchen with suds and disinfectant so John could siphon it into the vacuum; it drank up the suds like an elephant's trunk. She ran down to the second floor, turning its long snout to the walls as John reversed the vacuum, spraying all of Peter's apartment with soap and disinfectant, one wall at a time. Don, meanwhile, spread it with a mop then took the hose, freeing Mirium.

"How are we doing?" John shouted down from his position by the motor.

"Turn it off, will you?" Don shouted up, struggling to hold the hose in the right direction. Meanwhile Mirium had joined Peter who was attacking the walls with a scrub brush. John turned off the vacuum and waited for them to catch up, sitting on the top step as if exhausted from heavy labor.

It took the three downstairs only a few minutes to scrub the walls and ceiling and floors and then stop, appraising the mopping up job still ahead of them.

"Ready to rinse?" John called down, then got up again, emptied out the suds in the bathtub and filled it with clear hot water. He shook the nozzle to signal them.

They began to hose down the whole apartment now in short spurts, rinsing and mopping, then the floor began to flood. "Stop! It'll soak through the boards," Peter shouted up.

"Work fast," John answered.

Peter and Mirium hurried to spread the water with the mop while Don continued to spray. Then Don suddenly cat-called, "Hey, Pee-ter!"

Those were fighting words. Back in grammar school days Peter's name had always been distorted when the fellows wanted to rile him. They would rub one finger over the other and yell "Pee-ter" until he came after them, ready to fight. Hearing it now almost made him revert to childhood days and he turned fiercely toward Donald. It was just what Don had expected. He turned the nozzle on him and sprayed Peter's face with water. Then he turned the hose away again and laughed like a chimpanzee. Peter was about to advance on him when Mirium shouted, "Quick, it's beginning to drain through."

Upstairs John reversed the vacuum and Peter grabbed the hose from Don, hurrying to take up all the excess water before it seeped down to Elaine's. The vacuum quickly took up the flood and then he turned to take care of Don.

"All in good fun, Pete," Don shrugged innocently, retreating a little. "Honestly."

Peter thought it over and decided it wasn't worth fighting over. And suddenly, miraculously, the apartment had become clean and he was too caught up with it to waste his time on Don. He and Mirium stopped to admire their work and John came down to join them.

"It won't pay to paint it," John said, "but the walls are still fairly white."

"Now the furniture," Mirium said, leading the way upstairs to John's spare room where mof of Peter's things had been stored. She picked up a canvas chair and brought it down again while the others went up. Peter gave John a hand with the large Elizabethan four-poster which stood dismantled against the wall. It had been Peter and Elaine's pride and joy—bought for peanuts from a bearded Yemenite in the lox and bagel district who had taken a special liking to them. He claimed it had once belonged to Disraeli.

Don found the object that most intrigued him, Peter's squat powerful robot that now stood frozen in second position, looking like a Korean mantu about to exorcise a demon.

"Forward to victory!" Mirium led. Their procession tortured the exhausted staircase but they got down safely two or three times, leaving Mirium and Don downstairs to arrange everything in its proper place.

Then John began to connect all the old electrical equipment—the robot, the air de-ionizer and the stereo, while the others invaded Elaine's basement for the rest of Peter's things.

Peter knocked on Elaine's door. "Get dressed, we're coming in." Then he threw in the laundry bag so she could find her jeans.

"For Christ's sake, what do you want?" Elaine shouted, and hurriedly made herself decent, knowing she couldn't keep them out.

They entered when she said it was all right and paraded out again with the tings that had been stacked against the far wall. Peter lingered.

"Thanks for returning that side of the room," Elaine said. She wanted to sound put-out and hostile but it was hard to be unfriendly to Peter. "You're all dirty again," she pointed out.

"The place upstairs is clean," Peter answered. "Wait til you see it. I was hoping, maybe, that you'd want to sleep up there tonight."

"Not unless you'll be sleeping down here," Elaine said. That cut it short. He left again to help the others.

She had wanted to stop him with a word or two but a terrible fear had held her back. She could not verbalize it at all. She wanted Peter but she couldn't accept that wish in words. She belonged to Nicole. Nicole loved and deserved her. She had no right to leave Nicole for Peter just because he had happened to come back.

Peter had nothing of himself to offer—he wasn't capable of the sort of love Nicole had given her: not the act, but the attitude. It seemed to her that no man could offer love as deeply as a woman offered it. The very things that men found so exquisite in women, Elaine found so exquisite in women: first, the memory of the mother, which is common to all babies of each sex and which, henceforth, predisposes men to women and women to women as a part of nature; second, the greater feeling of freedom and power attained by the rejection of a subordinate role—the role of the female, inferior to the male—Elaine could be herself and could be independent of the need of male protection; third, the greater concern and attention and passion—so well matched to her own—which only women, only lesbians, gave. Having known such bliss, how could she settle for the dull and drabness of Peter?

Elaine told herself this, pushing back the knowledge that Nicole had failed to satisfy her and that now Peter had almost done so. She told herself this because she resented change of all sorts, because she was constant and sluggish and because, now, it was to Nicole that she owed fidelity and not to Peter. And because Elaine resented change she walked to the almost vestigial telephone and dialed Nicole's number.

"Will you come back? I need you to stay with me," she said. Her voice was almost desperate in its blank, automatic coldness.

"Why?" Nicole's voice was emotional, full of impatience. "Are you using me to get Peter?"

"No. I'm terrified of Peter," Elaine answered. Her voice did have terror in it.

"Why?" There was no answer and Nicole paused to think a minute then said, "I'll be right over."

Elaine hung up and found the world upright again; the threat of Peter had been alleviated; it was up to Nicole to protect her now, to decide for her.

The group came down for the second load and she was able to face Peter calmly. But he looked at her only slightly, like a wounded puppy or so it seemed to her, and she said nothing, so he said nothing as he helped take up the heavy maple Shaker table her dad had given them as a wedding present. The crowd went upstairs again and only Donald lingered this time, giving Elaine an up-and-down appraisal.

"Who are you?" Elaine asked hostilely.

"Who're you?" Don echoed. She turned away from him but he grabbed her arm. "Say, don't be such a bitch. Why don't you like men, huh?"

Elaine glowered at thim and pulled her arm away. "Get out of my house!"

"It's Pete's house, isn't it?"

"No, mine," she answered firmly.

"In that case, I'm sure ol' Pete won't mind." He grabbed her suddenly and pressed his hot lips on hers, then let go again. "Enjoy it?"

Elaine wiped her face. "I don't like affectionate mutts," she said criply.

"relax, chick," he said, "you're not God's gift to mankind, either." He walked out again, kicking the door to one side with an air of arrogant unconcern.

Elaine stood, confused. She wanted to fume but she did have quite enough cause. Don's aggressiveness had flattered her. No man had dared kiss her like that before—not even Peter. Peter had always been too polite. Perversely, she now wondered what Peter might do if she told him about it—if he might be jealous at all. He certainly wan't being jealous about Nicole, and this was annoying her no end—could she possibly feel secure about him when he was never jealous? "I mustn't think of Peter," she told herself firmly. But the memory of him, the feeling of him, screamed within her.

8.

It was a day of noise and confusion. Everything was being put back in place, as if Peter were now turning back time, eliminating one whole year as if he had never deserted her at all. A blast of Beethoven's Ninth with chorus announced that John had connected all five speakers of the stereo. No Elaine could not even escape memories by hiding in the basement. She put her hands to her ears and cringed deep in her canvas wing chair. Then Nicole burst through the broken door, dressed for battle in corduroy toreador slacks and a Mexican embroidered shirt of unbleached muslin and shouted over the music, "Come on, we can stay at my place. This is too noisy."

"No one's going to chase me away from my house," Elaine said, panic resurging inside of her. She did not want to leave the scene. With what seemed to be angry determination, she got up. "We're cleaning this place up and staying here." then, to emphasize her point, she picked up a hammer and pounded the radiator pipe. The hi-fi instantly stopped and Elaine put down the hammer with an air of victory.

"Why do you want to stay here?" Nicole asked impatiently. "It is much better at my place."

"I'm not going to give Peter that much satisfaction," Elaine answered, and slammed a chair down in a corner, away from the mess in the middle of the floor.

"You are being childish," Nicole sighed, "but all right, I will fight Peter here with you." She went over and made Elaine stop clearing the floor for a moment, taking her in her arms in a relaxed, familiar kiss. Elaine hung around her neck, feeling so wonderfully comfortable in Nicole's embrace—not filled with needles as she had felt when Don had touched her and not with the hostile emotional struggle that Peter had evoked a little earlier. No, it was peaceful in Nicole's arms, and the soft warmth of her gave Elaine a feeling of utter safety. She felt she would never want to let go.

"*Ma petite pou*," Nicole nibbled her forehead tenderly with a sort of nearly exasperated patience. "You are so foolish."

"I'm your little flea," Elaine said, clinging harder around her neck and pecking her mouth playfully. "I am butch, butch, remember?"

"And what do you think a flea is?" Nicole laughed.

"Look out, girls, the world is watching!" Donald burst in again, leading the clean-up squad which had now accumulated some next-door neighbors, the hose nozzle in his hand ready to squirt soap suds all over the room.

"Get out," elaine said, suddenly whirling out of Nicole's embrace.

"Uhuh, this dump's a threat to public health," he said, advancing authoritatively. "Okay, let's shove the stuff to one end of the room." Mirium took his cue and indicated the furniture to be moved so that John's hose could do its work. The crowd of male and female bohemians began to move like ants.

"But we want to clean it ourselves," Nicole protested.

"So pick up a mop and help," Don said.

"Where's Peter?" Elaine sighed, exasperated.

"Polishing up upstairs," Don answered, then turned away to give more directions, like a fire chief.

"Go sit on the stoop," Nicole said to Elaine. "I'll see that they don't break anything." Elaine submitted, finding her energy not equal to further protestations. Nicole turned from her and tapped Don on the shoulder. "How can I help?"

"Just hold the hose, chick," Don turned, taking her round the waist and positioning the nozzle in her hand. "Once the water's on it'll wiggle like a snake."

"Like this?" Nicole indicated, edging way from his arm.

"Not quite." He tried to advance again. She turned the hose at him and pressed the lever, squirting him full of soap suds. Don let out a yell and put his arms over his face.

She topped and laughed. "Like Freud, no?" But then she saw her mistake and apologized, concerned. "I did not know it was not just water."

"Get a towel, quick," Don clutched his eyes. Mirium hurried with a pail of cold water to wash out the soap.

"Oh, I am so sorry," Nicole apologized again, dabbing his face with a cloth.

"Ooh, you should be," Don said, making the most of her sympathy. "For that you owe me a kiss." He sat forward to take it but she pushed him away gently.

"Later, maybe," she laughed, "if you can prove you are passive."

"Alice, I just love being passive," he answered, sitting back for a moment to show her, then he got up again. "Come on, let's get this dive straightened out." He got a mop and led the clean-up campaign, pointing to the clear wall. "Start spraying." Nicole took up the hose again and the bohemians hurried to clear more of the floor to avoid spreading the suds on furniture.

Only Elaine watched, through the window, sitting on the stoop, and soon Peter joined her—coming down from upstairs. "Great system, isn't it?" he commented, sitting beside her.

"Ingenious," she said, ruffled.

"Want to see the second floor?"

"All right, show me the second floor," she sighed, "if you really must."

They went up the steps to Peter's apartment and he opened the door to his reconstructed Disneyland. Everything was back and everything was neat. The Elizabethan four-poster had its canopy and curtains all the way around and stood in its corner of the living room, a large private bedroom all of itself. In the middle of the same room, their table stood full-length, banquet style, with the long benches on either side. The far wall was decorated by the large, carved oak Florentine sideboard they had rescued from a demolished building and refinished. Elaine's paintings were hung on the walls, her good ones, giving needed color to the room. The stereo speakers, adorned with golden cherubs once scavenged from some elaborate paneling, gave the ceiling the added lift it required and masked the places where the plaster was about to fall. Their robot, fond child, waited at attention near the fireplace.

The scene moved Elaine's jagged stone heart. It was not only as it had been, but somehow better.

"Are you sure you don't want to come back to it now?" Peter asked, almost humbly, with a quiet voice that tried not to intrude upon the moment.

"Quite sure," Elaine said, but her voice wavered.

It was the perfect time to kiss her and he took her almost by surprise, like a praying mantis catching a locust, and she stood there, with folded wings, quite still, waiting to be devoured. Then she struggled, struggled to touch him and to respond, pounding herself against the hardness of his chest and arms in a passion that was all anger but could not, would not, hold itself back from the instinct to unite rather than destroy. Then she broke away and retreated against the wall, breathing hard and her eyes—frightened, pinpointed eyes—turned against him like bayonets.

"That's the way I like you, Elaine," he said, stopping, refusing to advance and prolong the game. "Don't you see? We're both choked up with anger. From now one, let's take it out in bed where it belongs."

"Is that all you've come back to offer me?" She was furious, shaking all over with rage. Then she froze suddenly. Mirium had come up the stairs, now pausing at the landing.

"John's gone to buy a turkey. We thought we'd make a banquet on your table—okay?"

"Great," Peter answered, not taking his eyes off cornered Elaine. "Where's the rest of the crowd?"

"Don and Nic are polishing up downstairs," she winked then went up the next flight to her apartment.

"I gather Don's running interference for you," Elaine said, recovered now, bitter. "Was that John's idea?"

"Just another wild scheme," Peter answered. "John's worried that I won't be able to patch us up before they tear down the building."

"John will never learn," Elaine sighed, then ventured to break the stare that had pinned her to the wall, trapped. She moved away and Peter let her, following her around the room. "Neither will you—learn, I mean," she said.

"Don't be so sure I haven't," Peter countered. "I've changed this past year. In a way, I've grown meaner."

"Please don't grow meaner, Peter—" She turned suddenly to look at him, desperately serious. "For your sake—don't be one of the robots.

"They don't allow horse-drawn vehicles over the Queensboro Bridge any more," he said. But then his voice wasn't hard: "Elaine, I've decided not to be so passive about my life. I've decided to fight that Army mess as soon as I can afford a lawyer, and, I've applied for re-admission at school. I'm going to major in education, futile as it may seem.

She paused. For a moment her glance was eager but quickly changed. "I'm sorry, Peter, I can't believe you any more. You'll change your mind again—at the first defeat."

"No, I won't" His voice sat calmly in the room, weighing on both of them with an air of permanence. Then he added, "Because I'm not leaning on anyone for support any more—not on John nor on you," He took her arm more emphatically: "Elaine, even if you decide to stay with Nicole, it won't make a difference in my plans. I don't need you desperately any more. I've broken the chord—my life *can* be perfectly complete without you." He stopped, not wishing to hurt her. "Of course, it would be a shame to give you up. But it's not a question of survival for me any more. I can find a dozen other wholesome things, and women, to take your place."

This struck deep at her pride and he saw it. But he wasn't saying all these things out of spite. He had to be honest with her at all costs. Elaine would always understand and accept honesty, no matter how much it hurt her. Being honest was the only way he knew to win her back. To soften the blow, he neared her again, hoping that she could see the tenderness beneath his stare. "I love you, Elaine. For the first time I'm really free enough to love you—not just cling to your apron strings for some vague emotional security I could never quite get enough of."

The iceberg was melting slightly. Elaine would have replied but John was coming up the stairs carrying a heavy grocery bag. "Dinner'll be ready in ten minutes," he said. "You'd better set the table."

"It takes at least three hours to cook a turkey," Elaine said.

"Not my way," he countered. "Now hurry up. Don and Nic'll be up to give you a hand." He continued up the second flight to his place, calling up. "Hey, Mimi, is the stuffing ready?"

"Aye. Aye, sir," Mirium shouted back.

"I wonder what kind of a gadget John's built this time," Peter said.

Elaine sighed and went to the sideboard for their set of made-in-Japan white china. It was dusty, so she brought a pile of plates to the sink and Peter went to help her. Then Don and Nicole came up the stairs, laughing.

"Everything shipshape down there?" Peter asked.

"Like Versailles," Nicole answered, then added, "before the Revolution."

Don had his arm around her shoulder and she was mildly tolerating it, playing a comrade role, undisturbed by the tense situation that might arise at any moment, when Elaine might decide to take a strong stand one way or the other.

"You can wash up in there," Peter pointed. "John promises dinner in ten minutes."

"Ladies first," Don said in a playful mood and promptly went in, leaving Nicole to wait outside.

"Hey, no!" Nicole shouted through the door. "I am still a

woman!"

"I'm only camping, Alice," Don poked his head out for a minute, then whistled at her.

"Nicole," Elaine suddenly called with a tone of impatience. It made Nicole whirl and she guiltily took Elaine's side, also looking uneasily at Peter. Elaine grabbed her arm. "Why are you flirting with Don?"

"I like his aggressiveness. We can hate each other beautifully." Nicole pulled her arm free, then took hold of Elaine's, strongly, conscious of Peter's presence but wanting to have it out in front of him. "How else am I to satisfy myself—if you won't let me touch you? Why don't you let me touch you?"

"Please, not now." Elaine tried to turn away, embarrassed before Peter. Peter yawned and folded his hands, appearing mildly interested.

"No, we will discuss it—in front of Peter," Nicole said firmly. "You are not a lesbian, Elaine. Lesbians are always passive, even when they are butch. You pretend you are Peter when you make love to me."

"Nicole—" Elaine wanted to argue but she couldn't find the right words. Her face was a bright red.

"No," Nicole said firmly. "If I am to be approached aggressively I prefer a real man, not a crazy mixed-up substitute."

"I guess that's telling you off," Peter commented.

"Not at all," Nicole turned to him. "I still want Elaine, but on my own terms. I want to be sure she is forced to decide."

"Then you're declaring war?" Peter asked.

"No, I don't like war." Nicole let go of Elaine. "Let us say we are both campaigning for a democratic election."

"The john's free," Donald called, emerging, and Nicole went to take her turn at washing up. "Hey, do I get my kiss now my hair's combed?" He stopped her on her way in. Nicole smiled a broad smile, full of loathing. "Not yet," she teased, "Alice."

"What's the first chore?" Don asked, gravitating toward Elaine. Elaine pointed to the dishes Peter had dried. "I guess you can set them on the table." She scarcely looked at him, her face still reddened by Nicole's bluntness and Peter's amusement.

"Righto," Don said, lingering for a moment as if he expected her at least to notice he was there.

"Pete." John poked his head down from the upstairs landing. "Give me a hand with this contraption, will yuh?"

Peter reluctantly ran up to help John carry down his latest contraption.

"Say, don't you speak to people?" Don said to Elaine.

"Oh? Are you people?" Elaine answered coldly.

"Hey, don't be that way," he complained. "It's not nice."

"Why in the world should I be nice?" Elaine said.

"Because I like you—the both of you," he bent over and whispered, motioning toward Nicole in the john. "Now, come on, let's make peace." He put on his sweetest expression.

Elaine was about to shoot him down dead with her eyes but then she saw Peter and John coming down the stairs and decided to begin smiling at Don, very broadly.

"That's better," Don shucked her on the chin. "Now you look more like a girl."

Peter noticed and looked at her suspiciously, but he was too occupied helping John carry his new masterpiece—a large glass-topped box that had all sorts of wires inside and around it. Mirium followed after them, holding a huge platter on which the uncooked turkey rested, stuffed and surrounded by sweet potatoes. The put the machine and the turkey down on the kitchen table and then Mirium went back up for the baby.

"I told the neighbors to come back later for a party," John said. "Everyone sit down. Dinner's almost ready."

"Sit? Hell no, I want to watch this act," Don said, squatting on the floor. Nicole came out of the john and sat beside him. Peter and Elaine remained standing, also fascinated by John's new toy.

"You'd better stand back, then," John warned, "it's not quite perfected." They gave him room and he rolled up his sleeves like a magician and began the performance: first, he took the stuffed bird and put it into the machine; then he took the sweet potatoes and impaled them on a long skewer and set the skewer rotobroil-fashion over the turkey. "Now for the cooking," he said.

At that moment Mirium joined him and handed the baby to Elaine so that she might be free to set out the cranberry sauce and the other vegetables she had prepared upstairs on their stove.

"Are we ready?" John asked, looking around him. "Stand back."

He plugged the machine into a wall socket, then closed the glass door and dramatically pulled the switch. Multiple short lightning-bolts zapped between the solenoids inside the little chamber and in good time, the executed turkey was well-browned and juicy inside out and the potatoes were soft.

John closed the switch and opened the glass door again, fanning the smell of ozone away from his nose. "Now, just one more second," he said, turning another switch, "until the electromagnet underneath cleans off all the static electricity from this bird, and then we'll be ready to eat."

"This may not look like the house of the future," Mirium boasted proudly, "but John certainly has stocked it with all the equipment that might go into it."

"You wait till you see the new house we're moving into—as soon as they start tearing down this matchbox," John added. "Plenty of room for everyone to hang out there for a stay." He looked at all of them, but especially at Peter and Elaine who were taken aback at the unexpected invitation. "Well," John continued, "everybody sit around the table and we'll start carving."

"You sit at the head of the table, Pete," Mirium said, taking the baby back from Elaine who as only too glad to be rid of her bundle of joy because Nicole was beginning to notice it.

"Oh, how nice. Is it a he or a she?" Nicole asked Mirium, taking its fingers playfully, barely noticing John's scientific experiment.

"It's a she," Mirium said.

"Oh, she's so pretty. Elaine, don't you like her?" Nicole went on.

"The world has too many children," Elaine answered dryly. Nicole shrugged to Mirium and Mirium shrugged in return.

"Madam," Peter requested of Elaine, "would you sit at the other head of the table?"

Elaine quietly complied and Nicole took the seat at her right. Don quickly sat at her left and John and Mirium sat at both sides of Peter. Mirium had put the baby down on a blanket at the corner of the carpet where she might play safely with her toys without causing too much wreckage around her.   She was still too small to walk and lay mostly on her stomach.

John had put the turkey on the platter with the potatoes around it, and had brought the platter to the table, setting the carving tools before Peter.

"I suppose we ought to say some kind of *Grace*," Peter said, "in keeping with the pioneer spirit—community dinners et al. Elaine?" He looked at her as being the one with the best religious background.

"By all means, a sermon please," John spoke up and the others laughed.

Elaine smiled wryly. "Very well, but you asked for it." She poured herself some water from the pitcher and stood up.

"Hurry up, the turkey'll get cold," Don kibbitzed.

Elaine ignored him and coughed. "To the universal fetus that has long since died of old age—as we are about to—" she began, then paused to think of the next word.

"Be serious," Nicole interrupted. "I want this to be a beautiful moment."

"I am serious," Elaine said. "Hush now, I'm composing a poem."

"Then compose one to life instead of death," Peter spoke up from across the long table.

"If you think you can do better, I am prepared to yield the floor," Elaine answered. Peter did not reply and so she began again. "This executed bird before us was once alive and now we cannibal it for supper. We eat of life until the day we, too, are eaten."

"This is making me puke," Don commented.

"Shut up, she's getting to the point," John said.

"Thank you," Elaine bowed to him. "Now, in honor of Caryl Chessman, we sit down to a hearty meal."

"No. I cannot leave it on that note." Nicole stood. "Elaine is always too bitter. I want to say I believe in the future—I believe that some day the world will be perfect, and all the people in it."

"Here, here," Don thumped the table for applause.

"And we'll be alive to see it," Mirium promised.

"Now may I carve?" Peter asked, taking the implements up and approaching the bird with the expert air of a surgeon.

They ate it down to the carcass and even Elaine stuffed herself, despite the threat of her ulcer. Then John poured them all some bathtub wine, compliments of the Italian family across the street, and Mirium brought ice cream and chocolate sauce and bananas for desert and then brought the baby upstairs to sleep.

"I would like to propose a toast." Don stood, already giddy from the wine. "To all the beautiful women in this room."

"Aye, aye," John said, and took up his glass.

Peter had been staring intently at Elaine. He took up his glass automatically and sipped to the toast. Elaine did not drink from her glass. Her eyes were on Peter but it was difficult to predict what she was thinking. Nicole, also sensitive to her silence, impulsively put her hand on Elaine's hand, squeezing it reassuringly. It made Elaine turn and look at her.

"I'm rather tired," she said. "Do you suppose we could turn in early?"

Nicole shrugged. "It's up to you."

"Don't go yet—we're about to have party," John said.

"I don't like parties, thanks," Elaine said. She stood, looking toward Nicole. "Shall we?"

Nicole got up reluctantly. But they were unable to leave. As if John had pressed a button, there was a knock on the downstairs front door.

"That's the crowd," John said, and ran down to let them in—a dozen of them, white and black, carrying bongo drums and guitars and bags of booze; some of them were high on tea, others were tourists tagging along.

"Go right upstairs, people," John said, pointing the way. Then he called up, "Hey, clear the floor up there. Don? Nic? Pete?"

"Pete? Well for God's sake, is he back?" Othello, a brown

bearded giant of a sculptor, exclaimed as he handed John his six-pack.

"Yep, Pete's back," John said, "go on up."

The black man rushed up, nearly breaking the staircase, followed by Perdue, his small blond wife who also knew Peter, and then by the bunch of others, some old friends and others strangers. There were Bernie Pollackoff and his wife Velma, who both painted; Billie Taulman and partner Diana Rhodes, two Un-Beat poetesses with a day-job in advertising; Icharus, the tall Watusi just back from Ethiopia bringing along a couple of uniformed airlines hostesses and their pilot dates due for a quick flight to Europe and back at 3 a.m. the next morning; two smooching college seniors with their sophomore tag-alongs; and Guillaume, the effeminate but un-"gay" folk singer from the *Rienzi*, surrounded by his latest assortment of young adoring virgins. The guest list kept on growing as the doorbell rang and rang again and John kept collecting contributions of booze and potato chips and soda, then delegated the task to someone else and led the way upstairs to help organize the refreshments.

The dining room table had been pushed to the wall and the floor was still being cleared. Mirium was up and down on short babysitting breaks with bunches of paper cups and was now injecting vodka into a huge bowl of white grapes, looking like a mad doctor with her hypodermic.

Elaine and Nicole had gotten up to leave but weren't able to because of the incoming crowd. "You simply can't go now," Peter said, stifling a smile. "Stay and join the orgy." With that he pulled the curtains back on the Elizabethan bed and plopped comfortably into it. "Won't the two of you lie down?"

"No thanks," Elaine said, sitting in the blue canvas wing chair at the far corner, assuming an air of passive resistance. Peter was suddenly affectionately attacked by three or four old acquaintances and couldn't get up to follow her. But Nicole sought her out through the crowd.

"Oh, please let us stay, Elaine," she begged. "It is so much like Paris."

Elaine shrugged, indicating her total absence from the scene.

"Take your pick," John said, coming to her with some bottles. Elaine chose a fifth of tequila, opened it and took a long, suicidal gulp.

Don reached over and grabbed a quart of saki. "How about a swallow?" he invited Nicole, tearing off the seal on the bottle. Nicole took a swallow, following Elaine's example, set to get lost in the spirit of the party. Don took the bottle back and drank his share and then wiped the sweat off his face with his shirt which was now open in front to expose his strong, athletic chest. He reached to pull Nicole to him, but she wouldn't kiss him, shutting her mouth tight and shaking her head in a no. Instead of insisting, he held her close, rubbing the back of her neck with his free hand. "Mmm, that feels good," Nicole purred selfishly and grabbed another swallow from his bottle.

"Grapes, anyone?" Mirium carried the bowl around with its subversive ingredient and offered it to Peter, who now shared his bed with Othello and Perdue, still sober and hopelessly trapped by their eager conversation. Peter took a couple of grapes and watched Elaine as she drank from her bottle, holding it high in the air with a mean determination to cash out on the party by getting good and drunk as quickly as possible.

Peter watched the whole party scene without really wanting to be in it—from his place on the large four-poster. He didn't like orgies any more—all he really wanted was Elaine.

The pilots already had the airline hostesses up against the kitchen wall, getting set for some quick stand-up sex between flights. Shielding them from view at the far end of the living room, Icharus was setting up his bongos and Guillaume took a seat next to them with his homemade zither. The virgins sprawled around him ready for a folk sing, unconscious of the miniature Hollywood roulette in the kitchen behind them.

"More grapes?" Mirium maniacally came around again. Peter popped a couple more in his mouth and the sharp vodka tickle his tongue.

This was a party that never ended, that just moved from house to house. Once in a while, some of the people would go home and others would take their place—and some, those who had no place to sleep or were far away from home, merely left the party by sprawling on the nearest couch whenever they got tired. Many of the temporarily homeless—the Mid-west runaways, the airplane and motorcycle travelers, the California tea-heads—followed the part all over town, getting a chance to eat and drink and exist without working, without prostituting themselves at daytime jobs. The tourists in the crowd—those who had homes somewhere but came along for kicks—furnished the bread and the booze and the pot and the occasional real piece of cheese needed to keep it going. Bread was important, especially to the tea-heads—bread was what the tea-heads talked about most. John always had a roll when he callled a party, so the bongo players would come over and stay as long as he wanted.

"Hmm, Pete, I just love your great big bed," Perdue purred, stretching out on it, her feet bare and her skirt carelessly exposing her above the knees. Othello put his dark hand on her white ankle and rubbed her foot while talking about the new Moore exhibit at the museum. Peter listened, slightly bored, his eyes always returning to look at Elaine across the room. It was nice to see old friends but he suddenly realized that he had changed considerably since last year: he no longer belonged with the crowd in this room, he no longer had a need for the extra kick of being "way out."

He had outgrown his passion for John's orgies and now felt as bored as Elaine felt, sinking ever deeper in her canvas chair, guzzling tequila. Now he ached to talk to her again, ached to impart some important piece of information about his recent inner growth. He ached to tell her that all this time he had been reluctant to really live life, to take the passing of time by the horns, in the hope that he could still hang on to childhood by refusing to begin the important things he wanted to do as an adult, procrastinating by losing himself in the party that never ended. But time had passed on anyway, in spite of him. Life had thumped on in spite of his reluctance to beat out the minutes with his pulse.

Elaine, too, had been reluctant to live—had tried hard to make time stand still by not doing anything important, by not feeling any important emotion. Peter ached to make her realize that there was no more time to waste—the great world of their dreams, the paradise of their future, was existing here and now; every minute the had already waited for their life to begin, every waiting minute was no a wasted one.

"Say, don't you like Henry Moore?" Othello said, suddenly stopping his discussion to find out if Peter was really listening.

"I think he's great," Peter answered, "but not now. I'm in a hell of a mood."

Othello followed the direction of Peter's eyes and saw Elaine and understood. "Here, have some Gilbey's," he said, "it mixes with the grapes."

Peter took a good, mean swallow and handed back the bottle, his eyes still on Elaine.

The bongo drums began and, with them, a cool sax played by one of the virgins. Guillaume's zither filled out the tune. A strange combo, not for jazz but for something improvised and surrealistic, slow, way out cool, like a Bach cantata on a forty-two-tone scale that send little Picasso pictures through the brain—perfect for snake dancing, the pauses being as important as the music—pauses that throbbed with silence and drove one mad, reflecting the slow world of the tea-head. But Peter didn't need pot to appreciate the imagery, the enhanced quality of the sound-details.

Nicole was sitting behind Elaine's chair, next to Don on the floor, drinking heavily from his bottle of saki. She seemed to be making a desperate effort to enjoy herself, looking sidewise at Elaine from time to time, paying remote attention to Don with an angry determination not to be unhappy tonight, not to let her world fall apart. It made Peter doubly realize that Nicole had given up on Elaine, had had little hope of winning her since this morning. He shed an inner tear for Nicole, empathizing for a moment; he couldn't help liking Elaine's mistress, had always found her *simpatica*. She reflected Elaine's excellent taste.

"Great party, isn't it?" John said, coming to sit down beside Peter on the bed, plunging his corner way down by his weight. He still had his sleeves rolled up now like a football coach watching a practice session—he and Mirium had been alternating babysitting with going about efficiently keeping the crowd supplied with goodies.

"Brilliant," Peter said without enthusiasm. Actually, he found his new role of bystander very upsetting. The airlines hostesses were now coming on schedule. Between them and the musicians, one student couple was draped around an easy chair, passionately writhing with all their clothes on, having sublimated sex. The girl, a dyed redhead of about twenty, possibly a Psych major, reminded him of Doris in the way she frantically pretended to be enjoying herself. The boy was a blond intellectual from the NYU Law School set who looked too young for his age and was trying to be a man. The tea-head circle, in a world all to themselves, were beginning their own ritual on the other end of the floor. A colored woman had gotten up from among them and was beginning a slow-motion exhibition, abstract rather than primitive, with a Zen approach to the music; she began to remove her clothes with delayed, hashished movements, first exposing her two full mulatto breasts, where the sun had not tanned her skin a full brown. There was no applause from the crowd—this was a quiet, intense gathering and noise would have disrupted the mood.

"Pure art," Perdue breathed, and the room got very hot and damp so that people began to take off their shirts and blouses. Don fully exposed his bare chest, lying next to Nicole, and Nicole took another swig of saki and watched the girl intensely with the appreciation and sophistication acquired in Parisian *caves*. The mulatto's lover had gotten up on his knees to follow her dance and his head bobbed like a cobra's, inches from her bare breasts. Nicole sat forward, her nostrils taut like a houng, and then she suddenly bent over Don and began to suckle the nipples of his chest, pushing his ribs with her hand to make them full and soft.

"Hey, that's googy," Don laughed, embarrassed, "try somewhere else."

"Quiet," Nicole said. "I am only tormenting you."

"I'm a willing victim, chick," he said, then pulled her on top of him, locking his legs around her.

"Behave yourself," she said, and squished a grape on his face dangerously close to his eye.

John, his shirt now unbuttoned revealing a thick mat of fur, restlessly got up and tended to the passing of more booze. The Maltese dancer continued to peel of her many-colored clothes, taking all the time in the world and exposing her sculptured bones and muscles in bits and pieces rather than as part of a whole—here a rib cage, there part of a pelvis and Venus-mount as her clothes swung back and forth before dropping. Her lover still followed below her, his hands now massaging her upper legs and thighs, warming her taut, round muscles as they moved. Then they suddenly tired and fell back on the floor where he gave her a puff of his weed.

The mood, the sweet smell of marijuana, were beginning to make Peter sick now and he looked toward Elaine who was by now catatonic in her chair, her bottle half gone. He wanted to go over to her but he didn't want to join the party and talking love to her now would only make them part of John's orgy.

Nicole got up and pulled Don with her, and they began to dance, taking up where the Maltese had left off, doing a Parisian belly rub. His bare chest was drenched with sweat and so was Nicole's forehead—sweat from the saki and the closeness of the room. Don's stomach, bare to just below the belly button, pressed savagely against Nicole, wrinkling the front of her shirt with the dampness of him. The music gradually changed for them to a more intense beat and the crowd turned on the floor to look at their side of the room.

"Hey, you can really dance," Don said, his arms holding her arms behind her, *apache* fashion.

"You are not giving me much opportunity to show you," Nicole said, trying to break away from him for a pirouette.

"It's much nicer up close," he answered, then suddenly paused and forced her still a moment, taking her mouth in a wet, drunken kiss. Instead of fighting she seemed to yield, and then efficiently bit his tongue. "Ooh you bitch!" He let out a holler and let go of her quick. She wiped her mouth with an expression of utter disgust and then walked away from him, going to Elaine. "Come on," she said, "dance with me."

Elaine got up, zombie-like, and let Nicole lead her to the middle of the floor, where they began to dance very closely, Elaine's head resting against Nicole's shoulders, her mouth pressed at the nape of Nicole's neck.

"Pete, don't mourn," Perdue said, reaching one hand over to pat his shoulder as he lay on the bed, his head on the pillow, watching the whole scene with a passive sadness gotten from too much Gilbey's and grapes. Othello was on top of her, his mouth on one of her breasts, and the weight of their two bodies was nearly breaking a leg on the antique four-poster.

Peter sighed. "I'm all right, really." He was still sober and very bored. He couldn't even feel jealous any more. He threw another grape in the air and caught it in his mouth.

"I'll show you, smart Alice," Don said to Nicole in a loud voice, quite riled now and emptying the bottle of saki with one gulp. He threw it out an open window and it crashed on the sidewal, luckilly hitting no one but disrupting the quiet mood of the tea-heads on that side of the room. He walked, staggering determinedly toward the dancing couple and separated them, starting to dance with Elaine.

"Hey, get away." Nicole tried to break in again.

"No dice, it's my turn," Don answered, easily over-powering Elaine's weak attempts to make him let go.

"Hey, Pete, are you going to stand for that?" John came over officiously.

"Why should I bother?" Peter shrugged. "Let Nicole sock him one." He sat up a little to better watch the action. Elaine was looking toward him rather desperately, too proud to call him to the rescue. Then she saw that he wasn't about to more and an angry expression came over her and she stopped struggling with Don, suddenly following his close, indecent swinging to the music. "Kiss me again," she said loudly, "like you did this afternoon."

"Say, that's more like it," Don said, and bent over her for a long clinch. Elaine's sudden change had floored Nicole—she stood there perplexed and rather wounded. "Peter," she called out, "are you going to stand for that?"

Peter had already gotten up, a trifle peeved at the turn of events. "Pardon me," he tapped Don's shoulder, "but that's my wife."

"Don't bother us," Don stopped kissing her long enough to say, then continued.

Peter clenched his teeth, feeling a little more determined, and forcibly disengaged them, pushing Don a little away. Don staggered, almost losing his balance, and then looked sullenly at him. "What's the matter, finally jealous, Mary?" He came at Peter and swung blindly. Peter ducked. Don crashed into the sideboard and his hand wrapped around a porcelain figurine which he threw wildly at Peter. It missed, breaking the other window.

"It's all right, folks," John said to keep the peace, "the wreckers are coming soon anyway."

"Sit," Nicole said to Donald, going to him and pushing him down on the sideboard with one hand. "You are far too drunk."

Donald looked at her stupidly, trying to figure out which one of her had pushed him.

Elaine pushed Peter away and walked over to Nicole. "We're going home," she said, trying to take her hand.

"Let go," Nicole resisted. "Go play with your husband."

"Come on, Elaine," Peter said, trying in turn to pull her with him.

"I don't need you to take care of me," Elaine said, shaking him off. "Come on, Nikki," she again turned to Nicole.

"But I don't want to leave with you," Nicole said firmly. "Go with Peter."

"I'll go alone, then," Elaine said, finding her tequila and staggering downstairs.

"Go after her, Peter," Nicole said, still holding Don down as he tried drunkenly to get up.

"The hell I will," Peter said. "I'll wait till she begs me." He went back to the bed and lay down, abandoning Mirium's grapes for the bottle of Gilbey's. Then he closed the bed curtains and counted himself out of the party, no longer curbing a yen to get good and drunk. His one consolation was that Elaine was alone, too. "May she stay that way the rest of her eternal life. Amen," he said, and drank to it.

Next to him, Othello and Perdue were lost to the world. Outside, around the curtained bed, the party was still going strong: the

California bikers and tea-heads were moving upstais for more quiet sex; the airlines hostesses and their dates were ready to drunk-drive back to the airport; Icharus had stopped his bongos so he could drink for a spell and the group of wholesome nonsmoking, mild-drinking intellectuals who had gathered around Mirium, now with baby cradled in arms, in the quiet side of the room were listening to the soft strains of a lute, played by one of Guillaum's virgins, as improvised accompaniment to Billie Taulman's latest Etruscan translation.

By the window on the other end of the living room, John was putting cold packs on Don's head in an attempt to get him sober, while Nicole stood by and seriously pondered following Elaine. Guillaume was playing a game of mechanized strip tag with the rest of the virgins by way of Peter's robot and their laughter and screams nearly drowned out the quiet poetry session.

9.

Elaine stumbled into the basement and shut the noise from her ears. It was all over the ceiling. She went hazily to the bed and took off her clothes, leaving on only Peter's white shirt for the night. The tequila was eating up her stomach and the back of her brain. She was afraid to throw up—afraid she might not be able to stop once she started, until all her guts were out in a bloody mess. She didn't want to die of a silly old ulcer. She had so much yet unfinished—especially the painting—she couldn't die leaving that monstrosity behind. What else did she have to finish? Suddenly the question presented itself and she could barely answer it—she had to finish life itself, life with Peter, the long details of daily living with him, the details that would make up the minutes and hours of her future. But no more parties, please! Vaguely, she remembered it might help to eat and staggered to the refrigerator. Then Nicole pounded on the door saying, "Elaine, let me in."

Elaine turned the latch and collapsed into Nicole's arms, suddenly very weak in the knees.

"I was worried," Nicole said, leading her back to the bed. "It is a good thing I came down."

"I need something to eat," Elaine managed to say.

Nicole went to the kitchen to get out the sour cream. "Peter's getting drunk," she said as she prepared a bowl.

"Let Peter get drunk," Elaine answered, finding a little more strength to speak.

Nicole brought the bowl of sour cream over and sat on the edge of Elaine's bed. "Why doyou feel so strongly against Peter?"

"Let's not talk about it," Elaine said, taking the bowl.

"We must talk about it," Nicole insisted.

Elaine turned her eyes away. "Isn't it enough he deserted me?"

"No," Nicole said, then waited.

"His body frightens me. It causes me pain," Elaine finally answered.

"That is not the best reason," Nicole stated simply. Then she got up and sighed. "Well, I guess I will go back up and find Donald. He's probably passed out."

"No, Donald hasn't," Donald said, appearing drunkenly at the open door. He staggered in and pushed it closed, then boldly went to sit with both of them on the side of Elaine's bed, trying to clear his head.

"You had better go back upstairs," Nicole said. "Peter will not understand."

"The hell with Pee-ter," he said. "Where can I throw up?"

"In there." Nicole pointed to the john. He got up groggily and went there, closing the door.

Nicole looked at Elaine one last time. "Do you really prefer me to Peter?

"I—don't know," Elaine said. She could not lie and even this was half a lie—she did prefer Peter to anyone else in the world, but she wasn't going to change things now.

"Elaine, be definite," Nicole pleaded. Then, not being able to control herself, she bent over and kissed Elaine's mouth, pressing her whole body to Elaine's prone, pain-tormented frame. Elaine responded feebly after which they lay close to each other, embracing, bathing in the wonderful comfort of being close together.

"Hey, great!" Don said, coming out of the bathroom a little less drunk than before. "Let's have a *menage a trois.*"

"There will be no *menages,*" Nicole said patiently, like a nursemaid. She sat up again. "Go back upstairs now."

"Come on, now," he lingered, hovering over them. He had a stupid, arrogant look on his face and his neck and chest were dripping wet from the cold water he had splashed on himself to get sober.

"Out," Nicole said, getting up and trying to usher him to the door.

But he grabbed her playfully instead, holding her in a bear hug and rubbing his body on her. "Hey, don't fight, relax. This is your big chance." he was wary of her mouth and instead, tried to overpower her with his weight, tearing at the zipper of her toreador pants. Nicole tried to kick him but his leg was faster than hers and he tripped her, falling on top of her and Elaine on the bed.

"Let her go," Elaine said with the strongest voice she could muster.

"Come on, let's all three of us wrestle," Don said, covering both of them with his body and trying at the same time to unfasten his belt. Then he saw that Elaine was half naked, covered only by Peter's shirt, and he let out a whoop, "Hey, a Venus on the half shell."

"That is enough!" Nicole said, suddenly becoming quite angry. She pushed him with all her strength and then bit him as he fell on her again, hard, on the chest. She hung on like a piranha as Don tried to push her away.

Elaine reached for the panic button near the bed—John's special anti-burglar device, rigged throughout the house to protect it from all invaders. The loud ring of the alarm went through the building and broke up the party, causing the tea-heads to get up slowly—as fast as they could but still slowly—and they began to try to leave before the police came. The intellectuals stood up from their poetry session, slightly puzzled. Guillaume stopped chasing the virgins with the robot. Icharus picked up his bongo drums, ready to be evacuated. And John, almost expecting the signal, took a bucket of ice and threw it over Peter on the bed, also splashing Othello and Perdue as they law asleep in each other's arms. "Hey, Pete, Don's raping Elaine," he said. Then he slapped Peter awake. "I saw him go down there. Get up and fight. Elaine's in trouble."

Peter couldn't tell if the ringing was real or in his brain. He woke up and staggered out of bed and down the stairs, following John's orders, bursting through the basement door like *The Thing From Planet X*. There he faintly took in the scene: all three of them, with Nicole pointing speechless to Donald—having broken away from him—Elaine nearly naked on the bed, her shirt torn, bending in a spell of ulcer cramps, and Donald, with his pants half off, blood streaming from his upper chest where Nicole had bitten him. Suddenly it all registered and Peter began to get sober.

"Hey, it's not as bad as you think," Donald said, suddenly feeling himself framed.

Peter wasn't about to be reasoned with. The world spun around before his eyes for a moment, and then focused into a drunken rage. He suddenly needed to fight—needed even to kill with his bare hands. This was the part of him that had lain dormant all this time—this was the rage within Peter Clausson. Donald looked like the grim ivy-league captain behind the bright lights, looked like the guy in the bar with the broken beer bottle, looked like everyone who had ever given him a raw deal—yes, even looked like Elaine, looked like what he might have wanted to do to Elaine if she hadn't always been so fragile and female.

Donald saw the blood in his eyes and stepped back, saying, "Hey, Pete, I don't really want to fight you."

Peter took a chair and threw it at him, advancing like a tiger.

"Wait, Pete, I give up," Donald protested. "Don't fight."

Nicole sat on the bed near Elaine, ruffled but rather fascinated by the turn of events. Peter threw another chair at Donald and it smashed into splinters on the way, leaving a great big hole where the plaster fell away.

"Peter, don't," Elaine said weakly from the bed.

"That's right, don't Pete," Don said, still retreating. He wasn't a coward, just lazy about fighting.

Peter threw a can of paint and it splattered all over the wall and

Don's chest, making it battleship gray.

"That does it," Don said and came at him. He was larger than Peter and obviously once qualified as a fullback. He lunged with a fist of stone that knocked Peter to his knees. Peter spat blood as Donald stood over him, the lust of battle in his eyes now, the reluctance to fight pushed aside by the ease with which he had been able to lower the boom. Peter shook his head from side to side, trying to clear the cobwebs. Donald, impatient to get on with it, kicked him viciously, enjoying the sickening impact, aiming at the groin.

"No!" screamed Elaine, "Let him alone!"

Nicole made an attempt to pull Don away.

Peter grabbed his leg just before it sank into his groin again and twisted. Donald crashed to the floor, Nicole scrambling out of the way. Peter was up in an instant, glad of this respite, of the chance to redeem himself in Elaine's eyes, yes even in Nicole's eyes. "Get up," he ordered, determined to win but in his own way.

Donald looked at him with cow's eyes. Slowly, reluctantly, he got to his feet and Peter was on him, punishing him with a left to the chin and a powerhouse to the body. Donald whooped, a huge, hoarse groan escaping him. Forced to defend himself, he sent rapid left jabs toward Peter's face in an attempt to keep him off balance. It didn't work—Peter parried the jabs, looking for an opening. He now felt sure of himself, *knowing*, as if it had all been pre-arranged, what the outcome would be . There was a new clarity to his mind; a keen edge to his purpose.

The opening came. Getting bolder by the second, Donald sent what was to have been the clincher—a hard right to the head—but it missed and the fist shot harmlessly past Peter's shoulder. Peter lowered the right he had been saving and brought it up in a devastating uppercut, snapping Don's head back, glazing his eyes and leaving him open for more punishment. Peter now chopped at his opponent, suddenly remembering another fight like this one, when he had almost killed a little boy—the guilt, the horrible realization of what he had done had made him unable to fight again, to really want to fight. But now it was different—now there was a desire to maim, to annihilate.

He wanted to cut Don's smug, leering face to ribbons.

Donald's knees gave way as the blows continued and he sank to the floor, crying like a baby and whimpering, "I don't want to fight any more, Pete. I quit."

All at once there was a return to clarity and Peter could hear Nicole's voice warning him to stop, and Elaine begging, and John saying, "That's enough, boy—no more—he's had enough.

Reason came back to him and he bent forward and helped Don get up, handing him over to Nicole who led him out of the basement, saying, "Oh, how awful. I am sorry!"

John lingered but a minute, knowing this wasn't the time for post-mortems.

Peter wasn't drunk any more, but he was groggy and his face was sticky with sweat and blood from his nose and mouth. He had taken his share of knocks but he still couldn't feel them—and his rage wasn't satisfied. He wanted Elaine. He washed his face and chest in cold water and then came back to the bed, standing over her. He wanted her now and he wasn't going to take a no again.

"I loathe what you just did," she said, looking at him with a sick expression on her face, as if she wanted to throw up over it.

"I did it because of you," he said. "Now it's your turn."

"Obviously," she said bitterly. "I might have expected rape to be part of your new, aggressive personality. You've finally joined the robot race."

"That's right," he said, unfastening his trousers.

"It won't do any good for me to plead with you—to tell you I feel sick, will it?" She lay there passively, only extreme sadness in her voice and face.

"No good at all," he answered, and sat beside her.

"I won't let myself enjoy it, Peter—" Elaine stressed.

"That's just too damn bad," he said, "because it's the last time you'll get me." He lay on top of her, not caring if his weight hurt her, and forced her legs apart.

"Please no, Peter," she pleaded.

He stopped her words with his mouth, biting her in a kiss that tightened rather than let go. He felt her struggle in vain under him and liked it better that way—liked it better filling her with pain. But he wasn't a sadist; he wanted her to respond, wanted her to want him, to beg for him. "Elaine, I love you," he said, suddenly becoming tender, "please don't be afraid. Be glad of me." He paused, not wanting to go on until she recognized his existence. There was no way he could arouse her, could call her to him except by words. Elaine had turned her eyes away from him, back to her favorite spot on the wall, and he could see the purple sun, her private, remote world, occupying all of her mind.

"Elaine," he called again, "don't leave. By all that's holy come back to me!" His words traveled the long distance slowly, and then the angel suddenly turned from heaven, came back down to look at him with vague blue eyes. She was crying, remotely, as she always did when he touched her, and he deeply felt the helplessness of being mortal. Patiently, wishing that he, too, could shed tears, he pressed his cheek to her wet cheek and continued the hopeless task of trying to make her warm, trying to make her human. "I'm not going to force you," he said softly in her ear. "I can't be that way any more. I'd rather leave." He started to let go of her, tearing himself away from all that he wanted most, from the warm comfort of her and the beauty of her pure white face.

"No," she said, and suddenly her eyes were seeing him. She pulled him back to her and wrapped around him like a cold and lonely child. "Don't let go." She shivered and accepted all of him with a willingness she had never shown before. And something else was happening for the first time: he was pleasing her, although she still fought against it with half of her still in the land of the purple sun—he was pleasing her in spite of herself. She gasped slightly and then let go of him, feeling completely at peace.

He buried his face in her breast, finally content, finally relieved of all his own sadness. But only for a moment, because she looked at him again and her eyes hardened into cold and distant Elaine again. "I hate you," she said. "I never want to see you again." Her face was unwrinkled, the mask of a defiled nun.

The words cut deep. He got up and sat groggily on the bed. Nicole was now pounding on the door begging to be let in and the noise resounded in his brain. He put on his trousers and opened the door and walked out.

"Peter, wait," Elaine suddenly called after him, but he didn't stop. Nicole heard her and ran after him, catching up to him as he stopped at the corner.

"Peter, wait," Nicole called.

He turned back for a moment. Dawn was coming up and the city was deserted. His whole world was suddenly a desert. He had lost himself, as Elaine had said—he had become one of the robots, one of the mean ones. It suddenly dawned on him with the coming of dawn and now he was sober.

"Wait, Peter," Nicole reached him. "Elaine loves you. It is very clear."

"I'm glad someone finds it clear," Peter said. But he had no anger in him.

"It's true," Nicole insisted. She met his eyes with great honesty. "We have made love but it was not really love—not as I know it or as Elaine knows it. She has not let me touch her—she has not been a woman to me. This you must believe—she loves you."

He paused and let this sink in. "Go back to her," Nicole continued. "I have no use for a crazy mixed-up heterosexual." She said it with a smile and slapped his shoulder like a comrade.

He let her lead him back to the house, then watched her go upstairs, back to the party that was a little more quiet now, the bongos having left and been replaced by a uniformed Irish tenor. From the empty police car waiting outside the door, it was obvious that the local precinct had come to join in the fun as they always did when John gave a party.

"Hurry up and go to her," Nicole said from the top of the stairs.

Peter ventured into the basement cautiously. Elaine had stopped crying and was lying with her back to him, staring at her usual spot on the wall.

"It's me again," he said meekly, "back to normal."

"Shut the door," she said.

He did so, then came to sit on the edge of the bed, timidly. Elaine looked at him. Her eyes were hard and angry for a moment. "If you ever resort to rape again I'll kill you in self-defense."

He nodded seriously, accepting her statement. She softened then and put a hand on his. "Please bring me an antacid?"

He patiently went to the dresser for the bottle and brought it to her. She swallowed one dry. "Luckily, my ulcer's a lot better, or we'd have had to repeat the hospital routine," she said. She was still scolding him. Then she sat up, finding it a little hard to make the effort but making it anyway, and began to unbutton his shirt. He started to bend forward but she pushed him back. "No, you sit there and be passive," she said.

"I'm sorry," he apologized, and let her continue.

"Do you know what was wrong all along?" she asked, continuing to undress him. "I never made love to you, Peter. I only accepted your love. I thought letting you please yourself in me was enough in return." She suddenly took his lips passionately, with her whole mouth on his as she had never done before. Then she hung round his neck and made him lie back. She sat over him, studying his face. "I'll pass up an impulse to sketch the surprised look in your eyes," she said. Her voice was low, throaty, middle-of-the-nightish. Elaine had never been like this before: she was actually human now, not some distant angel banished from heaven.

"I'm not sure I like you this way," Peter said.

"You will," she promised. "I haven't really changed at all." With this, her expression softened and she bent her head, letting her straight yellow hair fall across her face in glints of gold. "Peter, I do love you," she trembled, and it sounded like Elaine again.

"What brought all this on?" he asked, lightly stroking her hair with his hands. "This new you?"

She laughed a little, playfully tracing a line on his chest with her lips. "I suddenly grew angry, I think, at the world—for wasting me, for grinding me up into fodder. I don't want to be useful any more, I don't want to be a saint—I just want to live." She held him closely, her body covering his and pressing to him without fear. "Peter, don't ever let go of me!"

He held her tightly, feeling wonderfully safe about her—she would never slip back to that other world, back to the useless domain of the unreal, the unborn. "You're more of a saint now than ever," he said. "For a while, I was afraid it might be you that would be lost to the robots."

She kissed him on the mouth again, thirstily, and he realized that she was asking for him again, her body eager to receive him. He half obliged, feeling relaxed and comfortable about it. They had all the rest of their lives to spend this way. But now Elaine wouldn't let him be indifferent. "Don't you dare fall asleep," she said playfully. She pressed her hot body to his, clinging—not in desperation or revulsion but in a desire to share—to give and to receive. Now he knew that she was free of Nicole.

But the world would not let them alone. Suddenly the whole building shook as if an earthquake had struck Manhattan. Peter jumped up, prepared for the atom bomb. The second crashing sound changed his mind. "It's the wreckers," he said. "They're tearing down next door." Then he realized what time it was and hastily began to dress again. "I've got an hour to get to work."

The building shook one more time and the party came down the stairs and burst through the basement door. Nicole, arm in arm with battered Donald, held up an empty saki bottle and waved it like an abolitionist. "We are going to City Hall. There's a anti-Bomb demonstration this morning and we are going to sit on the sidewalks and get arrested. Come with us."

"I've got to go to work," Peter said.

"Then onward without you!" She led the crowd of tourists and policemen down the street, all singing *Onward Christian Soldiers.* Then John and Mirium, and baby-XX whose proper name was yet to be determined, poked their heads in the door.

"We're renting a truck and moving to the suburbs. Want to come?"

"Sure, after five," Peter said.

"Hang your job, boy," John said. "Come in with us. We're opening a television repair shop."

"And a health food store," Mirium added.

"Sure, after five," Peter insisted.

"All right, we get the message," John threw up his arms. He and Mirium and baby-XX went back upstairs as the wreckers demolished the next door wall.

Peter finished putting on his clothes, combed his hair and went over his chin once, lightly with his electric razor. Then he was ready. Elaine kissed him affectionately on the cheek and sent him on his way.

Walking down the street he suddenly had the feeling that the Elders of the world had stepped down and made a place for him. It was his turn to live now.

ArtemisSmith 1961

And Afterwards,
Came "Brother Thanatos"

opens   april   7
THE SAVANT GARDE in
a play which is a
HAPPENING for PEACE
A TRAGIC COMEDY
BROTHER THANATOS
by artemis smith
EVERY   9 PM FREE   MOST
TUES. & WEDS.
COMMUNITY church of n.y.
40 E. 35   YU 8 - 8373
zella bavarre
karen black
veronica castang
gerald cherkes
natalie chilvers
ann d'andrea
jim hill
lloyd hollar
james howard
mikhail itkin
dennis kooh
alan langer
judd laurance
michael matthias
jackie maxwell
john oken
sam overton
sidney porcelain
robert riesel
gloria ross
jacqueline ullendorff
mickey walker
peter wilson
michael j. yaeg
blanche ziegler
and growing . .

AFTERWORD:

Dear Colleagues:

It would have spoiled your entire reading experience if I had included one of my usual introductions, so I have saved my reflections for a postscript.

First and foremost to ease your concern about Elaine's physical condition, let me assure you that when she got to the suburbs and all of them finally connected with a proper holistic internist all of her physical problems were finally diagnosed by Mirium as a bad case of lactose and gluten intolerance easily totally eliminated by a simple dietary change.

(There was also the tapeworm Elaine had been hosting since her childhood as a member of a missionary family which was making her anemic and contributing to the magnificent pallor of her face and eyes that had made her so alluring to Peter. Once properly wormed and multipli-shot with B-12 and B-1, she lost her angelic gaze and all of her artistic visions. She ended up healthy, chubby and pregnant but not barefoot.)

When reviewers of the Gay-Ghetto community first got a hold of this long-awaited new novel by *moi,* writing as Artemis Smith, they reacted with shock, anger and frustration. What the blazes was Artemis doing, writing a straight novel, with straights in a happy ending!

Had she been brainwashed?

Had she sold out to the reviled Establishment?

No, at first it was not well received, but it soon became a runaway best seller for Monarch Books all the same—because to the *reviled Establishment* an entirely different message was finally getting through:

Folks,
OUT-OF-THE-CLOSET GAYS ARE NO THREAT TO YOU!

For Immediate Demolition, as my third activist novel was

originally titled, completed the panorama of my research into the alternate lifestyles of the late 1950"s. It filled an important crevice in the activist picture and explored intersexual relationships heretofore obscure because socially taboo.

It needed to be written because it depicted a very real, very normal, very contemporary state of affairs within the intellectual/artistic community worldwide - an underground counter-culture where "Gays" and "Straights" and "Illuminati" in the arts and sciences had long been coexisting in the open among themselves, perhaps for centuries - *right alongside other members of the Rainbow Ghetto* - for a ghetto it still was, to the rest of the world.[1]

Once in nearly every generation, some political witch-hunt emerges to wipe out an enclave of this type—which is why this was not a permanent sort of existence. Then the 'straights' would leave and blend in, and everyone else would flee and find a new place to hide.

Therefore this slice of life was a very temporary thing— decidedly marked "For Immediate Demolition."   But for those of my generation who lived it, for the brief time that it lasted for us, it was a magnificent moment that I (then also writing under the pen name of Diana Carleton Rhodes) and my partner Billie Taulman lived through in the 1950's.[2]

The book is light and satirical and meant to appeal to a much wider audience then only beginning to be bombarded by a sudden influx of pro-Gay literature increasingly free of censorship.

Its revival today as a play or a musical or a film would be nice! Any takers?

See it for what it is - a ribald and unbridled period piece of a time that should never be forgotten for it recurs in one form or another in

---

[1] In the late 1950's and early '60's, our Rainbow World was fortunately not yet contaminated by the drug culture that followed. Alcohol was the only excess, and most of us had learned how to handle it. *Alas*, not so the generation that followed!
[2] You may have noticed that I inserted Taulman and *Moi* into the background party scene together with some of our "Straight" associates who requested inclusion for the fun of it. Contrary to popular misconceptions, I was not one of the leading characters in the story, being happily married to Taulman!

every generation and usually in comic style. Its party atmosphere preceded and most probably influenced the productions of *Hair* and *Oh Calcutta!, Woodstock,* and all that followed.

Its message is universal: Gender Freedom for Everyone, Straight and Gay! It is a work of fiction precisely because even through its zany hyperboles it comes closer to the truth than any nonfiction novel can.

For the 1960's memoir that I am still writing to go along with the rest of this *Afterword,* you will have to wait and wait some more, then buy a few more of my books.

Meanwhile, let me end this with our continuing bid for a Nobel Prize[3] through the lengthy 21st Century Rainbow message Taulman and I have been trying to GET THROUGH to *BigDaddy* Francis I, *et al*:

---

[3] Hey, if you don't ask for something, don't expect to get it!

Big Category Mistake!!!
Gender is a material concept
which has nothing to do with Soul!
The Human Soul is a Shape-Shifter!

Guys, put these activist slogans on your tee shirts!

And to further elaborate:

What is the Shape and Fit of *Your* Soul?

The Unisex Movement does not mean Social Conformity to one and only one image or fashion, but rather the possibility of multiple forms of trans-biological co-existence—dictated only by the Aesthetics of Natural Selection.

But Now it also goes Further—to the Natural Selection made possible by the artificial extensions of Our Being—Our Cyber Existence, Our Polymer Existence, our Android Existence, our Nano Existence … and Beyond.

All of these new forms of Being have only become materially attainable in the past fifty years, but in the abstract, they have been anticipated since the beginning of civilization in the myths and fantasies of our forebears. And while the possibility of Human Souls enduring in some dimension out-of-time has been only a tentative hypothesis put forth by the various religions, today the continued existence of Individual and Particular Human Souls fully Conscious and Interacting past biological "death" may be made materially possible in the Information Age.

We can indeed, if we choose, look forward to actually—both spiritually and psychically—living forever, disembodied or not—or at least for as long as increasingly complex systems of data storage and retrieval prevail.

Popular Science Fiction has already anticipated all this, but not always as accurately as Modern Science now actually can lay out a practical strategy for its realization. The papers in my 2013 and 2014 *The Third Sex* Re-Issue anthologies represent a step-by-step record of the concept formation underlying the type and potentiality of our future-present—representing a quantum leap in Human Evolution so imminent that proper preparation for it is essential to each individual's personal continued survival—that is, for those of us who choose to keep our Souls as well as our Spirits and survive within it.

The difference between keeping one's Soul and keeping one's Spirit is analogous to the difference between participating inside the orchestra and being the soloist in a symphony.

The Human Spirit has always endured and sits as a background to each individual existence within a community. Many religions, perhaps all, recognize the existence of Spirit, for it is a community entity, passed on through family, ethnicity, and language. But the Human Soul (similar to, but not precisely equivalent to, the Freudian *Psyche*) goes beyond this.

The Human Soul emerges from Spirit but enjoys Particularity unique to each Individual and seems to be the outgrowth of Human bioepistemological interaction (cf. the works of Jean Piaget on the Moral Development of the Child).

The Soul is that part of the communication field that emerges from, refines, alters Spirit in ways that uniquely reflect Individual *affective exchange* within the Community. The Soul takes from and gives back to the Spirit, whether for the Good or the Bad, its unique epistemological record of acquired values within each niche and nexus of Society.

And as Communication breaks out of ethnic barriers, expanding the fields of Interaction, each Human Soul and its responsibilities and values becomes evermore challenged to hold steadfast in its Self-Conscious niche preserving Human Identity.

And so Godheads emerge, for the Good or the Bad, keeping an active array of multiple Spiritual identities capable of being summoned as armature against adversity. Many societies, such as the ancient Egyptian or the various Native American and Asian, embody such mnemonic iconography to keep track of multiple aptitudes for adaptability, much like the App icons piled onto a computer Desktop.

But the Soul is also that which is prized by each Individual as a unique Self-Consciousness. And for those Individuals who love each other, the unique communication had between Souls is not easily replaced by clones, or off-spring, or other DNA look-alikes, no matter how close the resemblance.

All the more reason to preserve one's Soul for as long as there are loved ones to interact with it! Now quantum computing and entanglement may actually be able to accomplish this.

But where?

And in what interactive dimension?

And for how long?

And what is to be done with Souls whose interaction is not valued?

Shall the rest of us damn them to Hell or Oblivion?

Can such negative forces ever be fully eliminated from the vast field of Self-Conscious Being?

The Information Age has made it possible for each of us to stand in God-like Judgment of others, and for each individual Mind potentially to be made a victim of that same hasty and presumptuous Judgment in one or more dimensions of the multiverse.

Imagine [*Your Consciousness*] trapped in someone else's informational matrix! Such a materialistic possibility is exponentially more dreadful than any local, or cosmic, nuclear holocaust.

Pandora's Box has now again been opened.

Be wary and Beware!

ArtemisSmith 2014

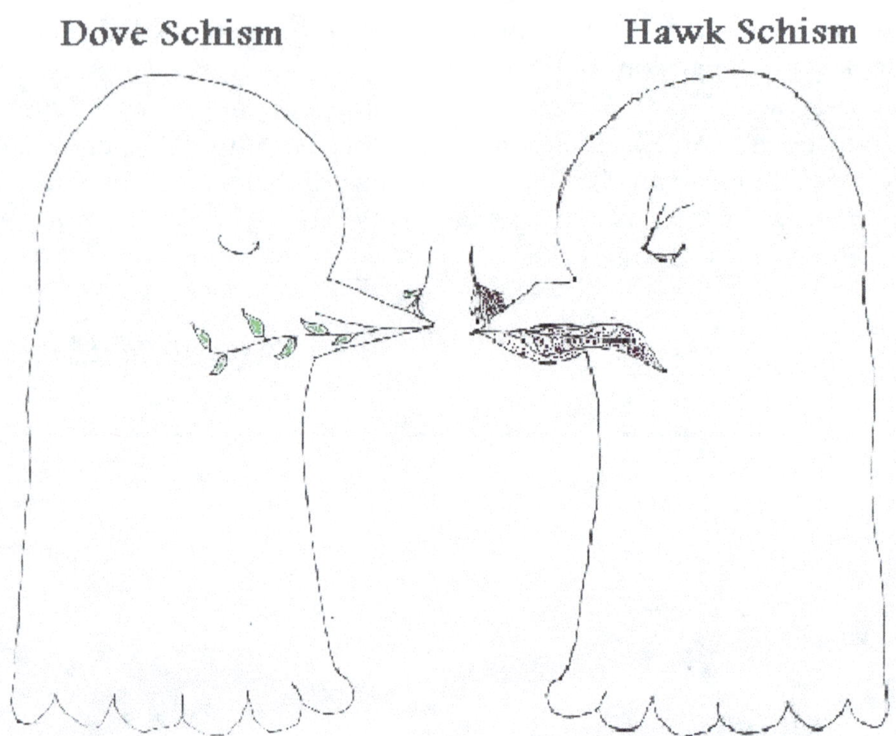

WELCOME TO
THE ANATHEISTIC CHURCH OF MUN

DEFINITIONS:

Our Church is the Only Church.

Our Country is the Only Country.

All Our Men and Women are called Mun.

All Our Gods and Goddesses are called Gud.

BOOK OF GENESIS:

In the Beginning was The Word.

And The Word was The Church.

The Church created Mun and Country.

Then Mun and Country created Gud.

Gud has sworn Allegiance to The Church.

Banner from "Brother Thanatos"

oil crayon diptych by Billie Taulman   c. 1962

… and Yes! There is also
An Appendix …

APPENDIX

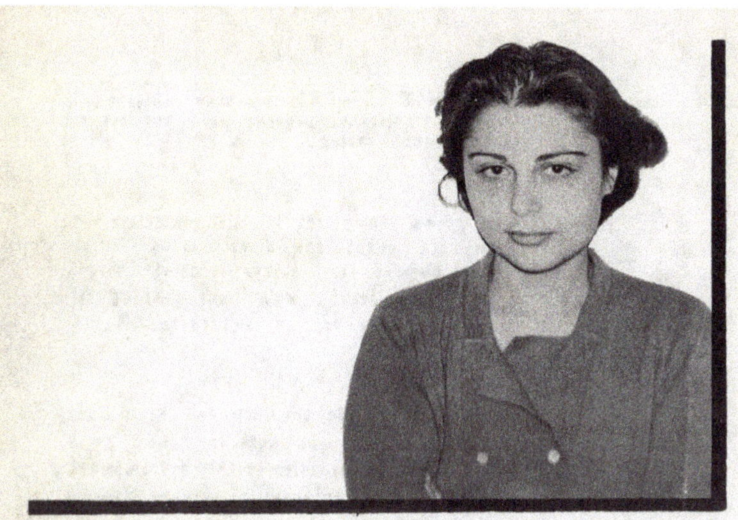
ARTEMIS SMITH
HARK
THE
PTERODACTYL
75¢

ARTEMIS SMITH has been published in paperback. Her avant-garde work has not yet obtained publication.

The poems and pieces in this collection are from her "notes and diary 1958 - 63," out of which her first surrealist novel emerged. Part of this period was spent touring fifteen European cities on a bicycle.

An ardent disciple of Gertrude Stein and e.e. cummings, her own work is marked by a sharp return to realism within a framework of ambiguity often recalling works of Rousseau and Dali.

stanley greenberg
editor
VAGUE PRESS

VAGUE INTRODUCTION SERIES
ORDER PREPAID FROM
333 EAST 70   NEW YORK CITY 21   APT. 9

THROUGH EUROPE
on a bicycle

VIERZIG TAUSEND SÖHNE DER STADT LIESSEN.
IHR LEBEN FUR EUHR. 1914-1918 HAMBURG 1963

As many Germans dead as Jews.

They were betrayed.
Build monuments.
Place flowers.

(No soldier thinks that he dies for war.)

Brave youths, I heard you march
when as an outcast child behind
a shuttered window I raised my
hand echoing "Heil Hitler."

As each child cheered a parade
let each grown man mourn all the dead.

No soldier thinks that he dies for war.

We who live thank Death for catastrophe.
(Make not the world Old again too soon.)
Each Private tragedy was for the Group
salvation.
(Let each grown man mourn all the dead.)
We who live are not without Casualty.
(Many of us were blinded looking Back.)

But the Few remaining who See
our New world
our Older new World,
blame Not the mistakes of youth
on One children.

Make not the world Old again too soon.

PARIS,
I find no joy in you:
here is one who still remembers
and it seems to me - that I
tread on the blood of princes.
I walked as far as the Tuileries
and wept.

LIBERTÉ   EGALITÉ   FRATERNITÉ

Let us all be of one blood now,
let us all be of one class;
for those who were not our brothers
are gone,
     those who were not our equals
are dead.

OVERLOOKING   ZURICHSEE

     The Meek have climbed the Mountain
     the meek have crossed the mountain

     and those who seized the Valley
               who seized the fertile plain
     though they nurtured it with blood
               draw from it only wine.

Oh my own Land
          how innocent you were
and will remain
    though with a sword you stand.

For to be at peace
is not to be at peace
     when lower than the mountain
               the mountain spring
mingles with the sweat of neighbors
flows on a heavy earth
an earth that covers flesh
          too soon returned to rest.

FLORENCE A TRIPTYCH

Cast down the spoils of youth
I have here a lifetime of years

                    filled with gold
                all filled with gold

                which I carry on my back
                        on my back

A fly has brushed my lips
and Love comes on Death's wings
clasping a pure heart in unclean hands.
Who will embrace the old, the ugly and the lame?
Come unto me, for I have kissed the leper
and left mine eyes with the blind.

You cannot tempt me with your toys
                Merry Christmas
There are joys I will never know
                no matter
                Merry Christmas
Let me wish you all the blessings
I have known
    enough pain to learn compassion
    enough blows to feel no pain
                only then will you know
how little malice I bear
how little malice

ROME A TRIPTYCH

<pre>
                    Orpheus
                did the gods
          so violently forbid your love
     that you have lost your eyes, your voice

        the eyes that saw more than the gods
             have seen and the voice that
                gently to the damned

                    imparted a hope
                      greater
                   than the gods?
</pre>

<pre>
           Nature says
      we have done no wrong

     it entrusts us with tender cares
   bringing the alley cat to whelp in the lion's cage
      covering with gentle moss a bloodstained stone

                in a wild
                unruly way
                stones make a mountain

                and though fingers of water
                dig out a canyon
                still
                it is a long and trial and error thing
                this great creation

                done without Will
                     without Love
                     without Mercy
</pre>

```
            We
      by our death
   have made desolate
    our ancient ways

            We
      have laid waste
       by our death
         our own
         temples

            We
      have yielded
       our pipes
        to the
       beggar's
         brat

         and
         now
         the
         streetwhore walks
         where once our muses
         danced
         where our decadent muses
         danced

         danced
   through our glorious
         decline
```



```
my life,
my one life,
my only life,
   dearly beloved,
mine all my life,
   dearly beloved.
```

ROME AGAIN

Wining children wring your hands
                    tear out your hair
Truth has died of loneliness.

It went among you on a winter's day
                    preaching more than the rose
                    more than the green of spring,

It came to warm you on a winter's day
                    its awful face aglow

And you yielded it a path
Yes you yielded it a path
                    as to a leper.

VIENNA A WALTZ
VENICE

Life
    you ravish the young
    the pure and the most fair
    you take the lion's share.

What were they all before you dunned?
Not harlot, thief or derelict.
Take from me nothing.
I have shunned your minutes of despair.

Life
    you cheat your saints
    of precious pain and sighs
    to live bereft of truth
    pure for all time.

SPAIN THOUGH I HAVE NOT BEEN

FLORENCE

From that high place
        we are very far
        from us ourselves
        as we were looking up.
It is the loneliness of kings we feel
        the loneliness of kings.

        Where to put oneself so high up
        where to put oneself.
            We sit posing like statues
        my beloved self no comfort to me
                            so high up.
        It is the loneliness of kings I feel.

To find another so high up
        another very far
        from us ourselves
        as we were looking up.
It is a claim of blood we feel
        a claim of blood.

        I bow my head in that high place
        feeling very small
                so small as a star
                so small as I was looking up.
        My beloved self no comfort to me
                            so high up.
        It is the loneliness of kings I feel.

CHORAL ODES

Turning to sun until eyes are blind
burns into sight an unchangeable
scene of earth and sky
        first breath and last sigh
        clocked by beating heart.

Taking of stone until lies are kind
turns into self an untenable
spoil of love and hate
        fleet change and lost fate
        locked in rotting skull.

There is no way where there are
        no sighs
    heaven is a thorny place
    but life is free
        in tomb
    from the damned
        unborn
    crossed by unencountered terror

There is no day where there are
        no eyes
    psyche is an empty face
    and mind is snow
        in womb
    come the dying
        ungrown
    frost on universal mirror

to joan mccarthy who died at 28

The editors call the reader's attention to the difficult rhyming scheme of this Attic form, to our knowledge, for the first time successfully imitated in English. Each word in the strophe has its parallel in the antistrophe.

Our living earth
                    from sun to sun
          growing forest
from growing tree
                    determines place
from star
   to leaf laced in a snowflake.

Are giving birth
                    in one by one
          sucking pollen
from sucking bee
                    entertains grace
from stay
   to leave lost in a forsake.

Or gaining worth
                    by won and won
          taking mountain
from taking me
                    ascertains trace
from stone
   to live left in a partake.

VIEW OF TOLEDO AS SEEN FROM A CROSS[1]

Three days I have wed a dead tree
(while my limbs grew to wood)

    nor am I an unblest debris
      rid of breath cold and ashen,
    pure in the knowing of me alone
      and not alone on that tallest pole.

    In a moment of grace, spare them
    this sight - for surely the sun
    was blind when the hail spent
    thick through the calm.

Three days I have bled a dread sea
(sins the lamb shed in blood)

    nor was it an unjust decree
      for my death and the passion,
    pure in the flowing of me at one
      and not at one with the meanest soul.

    In the torment I face, spare them
    my night - for truly the spear
    was kind and the nail went
    quick through my palm.

[1] After an interpretation of the El Greco made by Prof. Mirella D'Ancona of Hunter College.

                Life
                        that is
                                a fleeting part
                        sparrow.

        Wife
              that is
                        a beating heart
              marrow.

                                                        to b.t.

On the green breast of me grace your head
                on the cool moss
                not where my skin is worn.

My name is Earth that has by every man been turned
that has been one with every common man.

                Make of each seed   sunlight
                Make of each age   a mold.

In the brown crust of me place your dead
                in the cruel hole
                not where my womb is warm.

My prize is Birth that has by every man been earned
that will be won by every common man.

                Make of his flesh   fodder
                Make of his bones   a field.

149

in a PREHISTORIC ZOO

Now is the time of the glowing cat
                of the black-striped orange tiger
Now is the time of the great big growler
Now is the time of the cat.

Now is the time of the cat that stalks
Now is the time of the cat that walks
Now is the time of the black-striped dawn
                of the black-striped orange tiger.

                Hide all people
                        all pagans
                        all christians
                        all
                Hide under the rock
                        and
                    behind the house
                        all people.

Now is the time of the cat that howls
Now is the time of the dawn that growls
                She has you firm between her jowls
                        the black-striped orange tiger.

Hark
Hark the pterodactyl

   neither bat nor bird nor lizard
   from Heaven's gates loud-crowing
   bidding all to cease their striving
            toward an everlasting death

We are the stars

   WE ARE the stars

            gold, crystal and the sun
                all in our clay
            imprisoned in our cells -

               genes of the dinosaur

Be Not Afraid

            the god of death is dead
            he falls on his own scythe
            be not afraid

Walk the Road of Coals
Submit to All Desire
All of Heaven Burns in Fire
Be Not Afraid

            happy are the most forlorn
            the only damned are the unborn

Riding a train
Riding a fast car
   to get away
   to get away
   I am pursued
   I am pursued
   by one who races alongside
   by one who runs outside
                  outside my window

         over valleys
         over hills
         across rivers
         through rain
             and snow
             and rising sun

          running
          leaping
          never stopping
             though his heart beats
             though his heart beats
       and the twigs of trees whip his face

       racing alongside
       panting alongside
       panting outside my window
       running with bleeding feet
       never stopping
though I cross oceans with the speed of jets
though I cross oceans
       shouting to me in a hoarse voice:

                        " Nothing is impossible! "

The Day I Made The World
I held the Sun in my hand.

It burned my hand
    to hold the sun.

The Day I Made The World
I saw the Sun with my eyes.

It burned my eyes
    to see the sun.

(Now I am Blind and cannot See)
                    THE SPARROW

        I have no Hand
        I have no Face
        No smallish House
        Can give me Place

        I live with Pain and cringe before
        my peers
        I grope the void and only know
                    THE STARS

When I am gone, knock loudly at my door
(what awful emptyness within there lies).
When life is done, breathe deep my dying breath
(the hollow wind will chill your breast with cries).

From waxen crooked finger take my ring
To me no white and warm young thighs will cleave
I am no longer thing alive but thing
For me no strangers hearing grief will grieve.

There shall not be a moment's quiet rest
for ringing ears and searing bloodwebbed eyes
nor soft repose for heavy heads tight pressed
against a wall of heartless hows and whys.

My heart that was a bird is now a stone.
My name that was a word is now a bone.
                    to b.l.

Where is the Indian-priestess-maiden-princess
part of the sight?

The bowl is bluer than the sky you can have
that old-washed-out-pale-blue-smog-filled
                        even here cloudgatherer.

So these are the highest falls in the East?
I'llbedamned if they're not like an oldstyle
                        bathtubfaucet.

By Cayuga's skyblue waters hey
                        can we go swim?

In a slatecovered realm we walked
careful not to wet our shoes or slip where
the dawnoftheworld water had worn grooves.

                        TAUGHANNOCK FALLS, N.Y.

Go scrooge your round peg
into that hole and cry

    Dawn has splattered
    over all my maps.

I should worry?
I once cracked on all horizons
    spilling the milk of
    circumstance
    while you sat
    craving my left breast.

I once loved my maker
We walked in the fields
        and plowed at home
We never bottled dawn
        and looked at maps.

LOVE
and other obsessions

STABAT MATER

Child
     I too am a child.

     They said you were better off dead
     than charging windmills in a waking dream.

     They do not know you as I do.
     I press your ancient head to my breast
     asking: Do these loving hands
               for you hold whips or balm?

There was a time when I was blind
and you led me through paradise.
Searching in your eyes I found
        two azure thoughts.

I remember I used to say:

                    Your name
          is Honor.
          Before your upright form
          even the angel of death
          will bow.

Was it the Gorgon that you saw
or is the Sun now turning you
to stone?

                              to b.t.

My life decays in a coffin of air

    through wind and rain and
    hail and frailities of soul

Strangled by a chain of words
Swung from a breaking sentence

    while a voice out of time
    cries out its passion to my age:

"I long for a glance blind to living earth
I weep for a love lost before my birth."

What are bodies?

I will open my legs to you
        but not my heart.

My heart contains
        too much red blood.

A rose crowned in thorns
        will never bleed.

But I am not a rose
though you have called me one -
        nor am I a lotus.

A PARABLE FOR ATHEISTS

A man walked on a lonely road that cleaved
a wasteland wide as far as the eye could see
and farther.

It was a wasteland of brambles with leaves
and vines browning in the sun. Once in a
while a wilted rose, a small, stunted rose
would peer out through the thorns - but
mostly the brambles made themselves known,
stretching out even across the road so that
the man had to step over them, often catching
his trousers.

The man carried a shovel and a pail of water.
He was in search of a beautiful green rosebush
at the end of the long road. Others had told
him about it. Many had said that they had
known someone who had known a great farmer who
had once seen it.

This farmer was anxious to see it for himself.
He had seen only the stunted roses, the parched
and ugly roses. The water and the shovel that
he carried were for the care of this sublime
plant, to keep it green and in soft soil.

But the road was too long. The sun was too hot.
He found after a while that he had walked too
far to turn back.

And when he had drunk all the water and still
had thirst, he dug himself a grave.

            no
she is no longer here no more
hallowed and hollow is the hole
    the wh
          hole is the memory
    and her only soul

                              to rosemarie spier

Walls keep things out.
I built a wall once,
    built it high against the world.

You came and broke it.
I repaired it.

                              to robert frost

I have seen a headless doll

          nurse its own breast
          its own empty breast

(Sanctify Thy Suffering Unto Thee)

                              THE CLOISTERS, NEW YORK

This collection is dedicated

to the paintings of Vilna Jorgen,

to the lectures of Prof. Pearl C. Wilson,

and to Billie Taulman,

    who is a better poet.

The format and typography were designed
and set by my own hand, with last-minute
revisions made directly on the reproduct-
ion copy. Body type was reproduced from
my Royal standard typewriter.

This edition is therefore to be considered
the author's ms.

                Artemis Smith

THIS IS COPY NO: 1

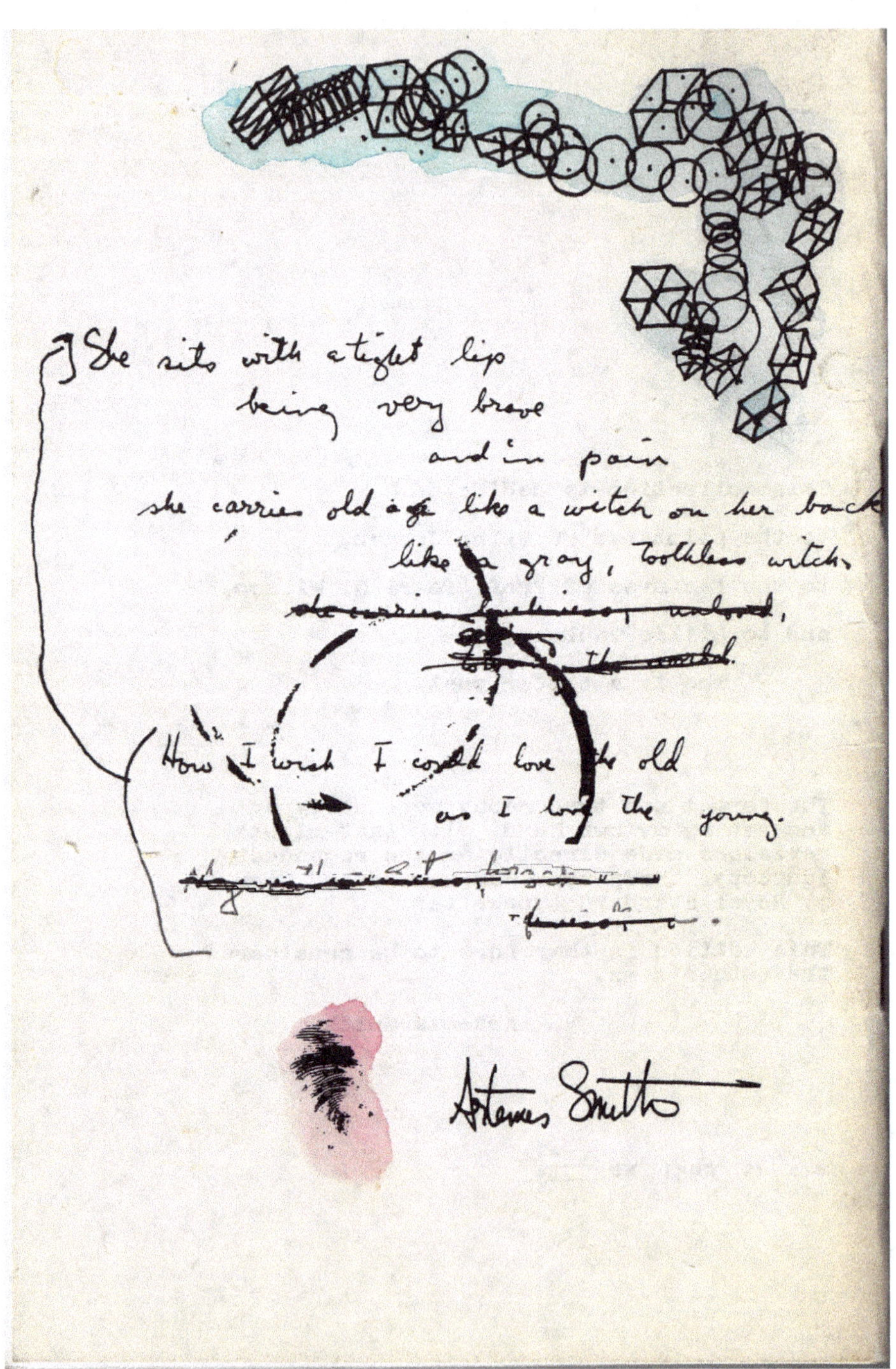
She sits with a tight lip
being very brave
and in pain
she carries old age like a witch on her back
like a gray, toothless witch.

How I wish I could love the old
as I love the young.

Artemis Smith

"Fecundity" clay model for a 30-foot Venus by VilnaJorgen 1933
"Mamma's Celebration of My Conception"

"Fecundity" clay model for a 30-foot Venus by VilnaJorgen 1933
"Mamma's Celebration of My Conception"

"Fecundity" clay model for a 30–foot Venus by VilnaJorgen 1933
"Mamma's Celebration of My Conception"

ART COLLECTION FOR SALE

Works by ArtemisSmith, B. Taulman, VilnaJorgen, etc.
For Benefit Sale to THE SAVANT GARDE INSTITUTE
Asking $200,000,000 + + +

DECISION

Originally shown as #1., Raskolnikoff, at her
1937 Rome debut exhibit, this work
was purchased by the Moscow Art Museum
and cast in bronze. Before casting,
Vilna had two plaster copies made,
one of which is seen here and retitled
"Decision".

Note the expressionist and unisex quality
of the work, which may have been
begun by her as a self-portrait.

Vilna's early strict Lutheran upbringing had
left her with a heavy burden of 'original sin'
which impelled many of her early works.

"Decision" Expressionist Unisex Self–Portrait by VilnaJorgen 1932

Layouts for a Modern Palazzo

in the ArtemisSmith Archive at

New York Public Library at

Jefferson Market

425 Avenue of the Americas (at 10th Street)

1965 AVANT GARDE MARATHON PHOTO BY JOHN GRAHAM

"John, oh John, where are you? Tried to find you, to publish your whole collection. You are probably dead by now!"

ArtemisSmith 2014

artemis smith

alive and well
and producing in
The Hamptons, USA

holocaust refugee,
multinational poet,
novelist, playwright,
human rights activist,
futurist and philosopher
of science

www.ArtemisSmith.net
www.Morpurgo.org
www.savantgarde.net
www.TheHamptons.org

an architect of the
human rights movements of the
1950's and '60's

Born:
Baroness Annaselma
Larsen-Nilsen-Vinje
Morpurgo in Rome,
Italy, 1934.

download some of the
key works of this
underground multimedia
poet and philosopher
who was blacklisted
for four decades for
her early activism in
defense of feminism
and integrationism.

coined and
stylized
the 1950's
Unisex
and
Unirace
Movements

1949
founded the
Savant Garde Movement
and its ethic of
inclusion

1965
gave the first
history–making
'Come out of the Closet'
speech to the
gay activist community

opposed the 1960's
and 70's drug culture takeover
of the avant garde arts

1982 - 1988
published and produced
the first computer desk-top
on-demand novels

1966 - 1973
authored the first explanatory model
of human consciousness contiguous
with the languages of information science

1973 - 1976
sued a major segment of
the academic-industrial
complex to accelerate
affirmative action

morpurgo@msn.com